W9-AUD-929

WEATHERHEAD BOOKS ON ASIA

Weatherhead East Asian Institute, Columbia University

Literature

David Der-wei Wang, Editor

Ye Zhaoyan, Nanjing 1937: *A Love Story, translated by Michael Berry (2003)*

Oda Makato, The Breaking Jewel, *translated by Donald Keene (2003)*

Han Shaogong, A Dictionary of Maqiao, *translated by Julia Lovell (2003)*

Takahashi Takako, Lonely Woman, *translated by Maryellen Toman Mori (2004)*

Chen Ran, A Private Life, *translated by John Howard-Gibbon (2004)*

Eileen Chang, Written on Water, *translated by Andrew F. Jones (2004)*

Writing Women in Modern China: The Revolutionary Years, 1936–1976,
  edited by Amy D. Dooling (2005)

Han Bangqing, The Sing-song Girls of Shanghai, *first translated by Eileen Chang,
  revised and edited by Eva Hung (2005)*

Loud Sparrows: Contemporary Chinese Short-Shorts, *translated and edited by Aili Mu,
  Julie Chiu, and Howard Goldblatt (2006)*

Hiratsuka Raichō, In the Beginning, Woman Was the Sun, *translated by Teruko Craig (2006)*

Zhu Wen, I Love Dollars and Other Stories of China, *translated by Julia Lovell (2007)*

Kim Sowŏl, Azaleas: A Book of Poems, *translated by David McCann (2007)*

For a complete list see page 151

Horses,
Horses,
in the End
the Light
Remains
Pure

—

WEATHERHEAD

BOOKS ON ASIA

Hideo
Furukawa
—
Horses,
Horses,
in the End
the Light
Remains
Pure
—

Translated by Doug Slaymaker
with Akiko Takenaka

A TALE
THAT
BEGINS
WITH
FUKUSHIMA

COLUMBIA UNIVERSITY PRESS   NEW YORK

Columbia University Press
Publishers Since 1893
New York   Chichester, West Sussex
cup.columbia.edu
English-language edition copyright © 2016 Columbia University Press
Originally published as *Umatachiyo, Soredemo Hikari wa Muku de.*
Copyright © 2011 by Hideo Frukawa.
English translation rights arranged with Hideo Furukawa through
Japan UNI Agency, Inc.

Library of Congress Cataloging-in-Publication Data
Names: Furukawa, Hideo, 1966- author. | Slaymaker, Douglas,
    translator. | Takenaka, Akiko, 1965- translator.
Title: Horses, horses, in the end the light remains pure : a tale that
    begins with Fukushima / Hideo Furukawa ; translated by Doug
    Slaymaker with Akiko Takenaka.
Other titles: Umatachi yo, sore demo hikari wa muku de. English
Description: New York : Columbia University Press, [2016] | Series:
    Weatherhead books on Asia | Description based on print version
    record and CIP data provided by publisher; resource not viewed.
Identifiers: LCCN 2015049578 (print) | LCCN 2015044778 (ebook) |
    ISBN 9780231542050 () | ISBN 9780231178686 (cloth : acid-free
    paper) | ISBN 9780231178693 (pbk. : acid-free paper) |
    ISBN 9780231542050 (e-book)
Subjects: LCSH: Tohoku Earthquake and Tsunami, Japan, 2011—
    Fiction. | Fukushima-ken (Japan)—Fiction.
Classification: LCC PL870.R85 (print) | LCC PL870.R85 U4313 2016
    (ebook) | DDC 895.63/6—dc23
LC record available at http://lccn.loc.gov/2015049578

c 10 9 8 7 6 5 4 3 2 1
p 10 9 8 7 6 5 4 3 2 1

Cover design: Catharine Casalino.
Cover image: © Fotolia.

Contents

Horses,
Horses,
in the End
the Light
Remains
Pure

—

THERE'S this scene:

An older brother questions his younger brother. He wants to know,

—What if there were this extraterrestrial, and the extraterrestrial is riding in a UFO, and this UFO is outfitted with a stereo system; what kind of music would you have the extraterrestrial play? Flying through the air, there, what would you want him to listen to?

The younger brother cannot answer, so he changes the question.

—What if there were this extraterrestrial, and they are in their UFO, and you could pick just one Beatles song for them to listen to, what would you pick?

Younger brother answers immediately: "Strawberry Fields Forever"; the answer suggests no other possibility.

"Strawberry Fields": the name of an orphanage that really existed in Liverpool, the harbor town that looks out on the Irish Sea. An orphans' song. A song of the orphans maybe, certainly for the orphans.

An open atlas brought the scene to mind. The scene calls up many related emotions. Not a map of England. It had nothing to do with England, or even Europe, nor North America. It is a 1:140,000 scale map of a place labeled "Nihonmatsu." The city of Nihonmatsu occupies the center. But I wasn't looking at the center of the map but up to the north and east. In the upper right-hand corner of the open page, along Route 114, you can find the "UFO Friendship Center." Everyone who lives there calls Route 114 the "Tomioka Highway." There is a "UFO Road" close to the UFO Friendship Center, complete with statues of extraterrestrials, according to the explanation in red letters. I read the whole thing. I read the whole thing, my gaze stopping on the place name and the explanation. That's what called up this scene. The scene of the two brothers. Right then, seemed like the most natural thing in the world, I knew I had to go there. The next instant, I rejected that decision. What was I hoping for? What I hoped for in that instant was for the statues of the extraterrestrials to be toppled, to be crushed, reduced to shards scattered and broken across the landscape. Wanted them pulverized rather than not pulverized. I closed the atlas.

Closed it with a sharp slap.

Or maybe a softer rustle like the flapping of a great bird's wings.

The UFO Friendship Center might be within the Fukushima city limits, or maybe it was Kawamata City, or maybe some other city. I didn't double-check. Anyhow, north of Nihonmatsu, then east.

East, then north. I can't forget that original scene. I am unable to forget it. Two brothers. The younger brother responds to the elder without hesitation. "Strawberry Fields Forever." Once the song starts in your head, it won't stop. I hear it now. I may be hearing it forever. "Forever." It's a scene from a novel. And I'm the author of the novel.

"North" plus "east" adds up to Tohoku, as in the prefectures of northeast Japan, which is what "Tohoku" means.

There's the voice again. It overlaps with the song. A clear command: "*Go there.*"

Eyes must be closeable. It's a characteristic of sight. It's what fundamentally sets it apart from hearing. Eardrums have no lids. But retinas are outfitted with eyelids. So it should be easy; you'd think, but I can't do it. I keep staring at the television; now the surface of my eyeballs is totally dried out. More like the dam has burst, actually. Teardrops fall. They are dripping like rain. How many times can it occur in an hour? Frequency can't be ascertained. "One hour," the unit of measurement disappears. Not twenty-four of them in a day. Commercials have disappeared from the TV. Delimiters disappeared. Things that cannot happen in the mere span of one day are happening, expanding— *expanding, proliferating, on and on.* The only phrase I can think of that captures the experience: "time is extinguished." To phrase it more concretely, consciousness of the date on the calendar, the day of the week, has collapsed. I think I can put a name to it: "Spirited away." Abducted by spirits. When a person is spirited away, seven days are experienced as half a year; three months feel like a matter of seconds. Time can't be accounted for, it's impossible to measure. I wrote about being "spirited away" in a novel. You know which novel, *that* novel.

Here's another scene. It's also related to a Beatles song.

The younger brother is asking the older: "What song is it, the one where the gull cries. You know, the one where you hear the seabirds in the intro, which one is that?" Older brother has an answer: "Tomorrow Never Knows." They used a tape loop so that the psychedelic song had an effect that sounded like seagulls. Both of them know about this, about these seagulls— known as "sea cats," actually—that sound like mewing cats, with their breeding ground up on the coast of Sanriku. They know all about it. And both of them are remembering the time they set off for the harbor town of Miyako up in Iwate Prefecture. Who knows why, but the younger brother remembers only the fierce birds, the kites, that gathered there. "In Miyako," he starts to say to the older brother, but older brother cuts him off, "Nope, we also saw the gull-like birds they call sea cats."

They went straight through Miyako.

On one of the roads taking them through to the next prefecture.

Which took them into the six northern provinces, to Tohoku.

I passed through there too. Just like the brothers, I saw Miyako, and also traveled up north past the Sanriku coast, and stayed one night in some budget hotel, just to be able to describe that scene. That scene with the two brothers. I still remember all those birds, black kites, nothing if not fierce. Like they owned the town. But I am staring at the TV, watching the news, and *that* Miyako is not to be seen. The town has disappeared. The elevated roadway there is probably Route 45. I have a vague memory of it being laid out like that. Everyone up there called Route 45 "the Beach Road." I wonder if there is anything else recognizable. I open the atlas again. I run my eyes down the coastline. I wonder if the line on the map is still true to the actual coastline. Impossible. Wondering about things in Jōdogahama? Geez, makes me want to rain curses on such a place name: Jōdo? As in "the Pure Land"? Where's the heaven in that?

Such a place now seems far away.

Infinitely far, I'm thinking now. I am remembering the scene but my brain won't call up the melody for "Tomorrow Never Knows." It continues, "Forever," on repeat. "Strawberry Fields" brings to mind the sea breeze. I remember the Miyako harbor and the Hei River. This all feels wrong.

I close the atlas with my thumb between the pages.

It closes with just a whimper of a sound. Iwate Prefecture, Miyagi Prefecture to the south of that, south of that, Fukushima Prefecture. Even without the map everyone knows the shore continues, on and on. I can't get the two brothers out of my mind. On and on, I can't. I gave animal names to the two of them. The novelist who gave them those names was, well, me. They have *inu*—dog—in their last names, and their first names? One is *ushi*—cow—and the other is *hitsuji*—sheep.

I experienced one day as though it was a week. Or three days that felt like a month. This is how "spirited-away time" works. I was not the only one that lost all sense of days of the week, I was not the only one for whom the dates of the calendar disappeared. (Everyone I was talking with seemed to be experiencing the same thing.) Meantime, everyone living outside the places deemed a "disaster zone" was able to escape the "spirited-away time"; I was one of those people. At the end of the ongoing and repeated announcements about the situation that "exceeds all expectations," we entered a phase more of stagnation than progress. Not a particularly exciting conclusion. At that point I canceled two projects. Given that I am a novelist, my work is writing novels. One project was a monthly serialization, the other was an installment of a serialized novel that had already been commissioned and for which the publication schedule had already been planned months into the future.

But the answer was clear. No way I could write.

Right before beginning this manuscript, it came to me. I had not taken a break from writing for as long as I can remember; never gave it a thought. There has not been a day in which I did not write, for many years now. I have no concept of a day off. Stop and think about it: I have been averaging three novels a year for a long time. And even in the periods when, you might point out, I only produced one volume, that volume was five or six times as long as any normal novel. Given the sheer size of the thing it was impossible to simply refer to it as a "long novel." I called it a "mega-novel."

But why did I continue writing like this? An internal necessity, drive, compulsion. Relentless.

That's just how it was. No other way to express it. I mean, I had just canceled two projects. Fiction, or anything that requires planning and then writing, was out of the question. I couldn't write. I couldn't see my way to writing. OK, not exactly unable to write. I experimented with some short things. Even while locked away in the midst of the "spirited-away time," if requests came in, I would write pieces for magazines and newspapers. As long as I could believe my words might have some direct impact I would give it all I had and pull out what I was thinking. I never thought that literature is useless. No doubts about that. The problems came with genre. If prose was requested, then what kind of prose? In what style? For what imagined readership? All these years I feel like I have been writing novels for anybody, everybody. No imagined reader in mind. That approach was no longer going to work.

I began writing this essay on April 11, 2011. I was about ten pages in when there was an aftershock off the coast of Fukushima. Just over magnitude six.

Every time there was a strong aftershock, I would revise.

The aftershocks left no options. A clear voice: "Revise completely and thoroughly."

Same voice as that earlier voice that said: "Go there." So I followed the voice, waited for some things to fall into place, and started writing this. When the flow of things gets stopped up, sometimes you have to devise a way through. So I fashioned one. A month had passed from March 11, 2011; I started thinking. Having written down the dates I started thinking. I first wrote dates according to the Western calendar. The Western calendar seemed the most normal way of starting. Maybe because the damage was global in scope. The international support was encouraging (to all of us Japanese, whether inside or outside the damaged area). But I had written a novel that never once referenced the Western calendar. I had written this mega-novel that only used the imperial reign years to mark dates. It's that one, that mega-novel. Even though it looked like a historical novel, I only used the imperial reign years. The publication date of the novel was recorded with the reign name: Heisei 20. The reason will be obvious: the first year of the Meiji era inaugurated a new system of assigning one reign name per emperor. In order to keep up a continual reference to the emperor system, I avoided using the Western calendar in the tale. At that time the voice commanded complete expulsion. Now, that doesn't mean 100 percent disregard for the Christian calendar, of course. I talked about the Bible in that novel; from the beginning I referenced Christ's family tree, and I kept it up obsessively. Even the title of the novel —"The Holy Family"—touches on it. Christianity, down to the details of Christ's family tree. The origin of that mega-novel *The Holy Family* comes from the Holy Family that is so important in Christian art.

Wait: I unconsciously capitalized those two words, written here in English: Holy Family. Never noticed that before: the two letters standing out at the beginning of the words—HF— resonate with my own name, are my initials. There's a surprise. Whatever; doesn't matter.

If the Bible gives birth to lineages and gives birth to myths, what are the comparable "holy writings" of Japan? The *Kojiki* maybe? The first part of it consists of myths, the latter part of imperial lineages. In that sense it is Japan's "Bible." In that mega-novel *The Holy Family* I only briefly touch on the early Japanese texts like the *Kojiki* and *Nihonshoki*. I really don't touch on the *Kojiki* at all. Know why? Because the *Kojiki* is about bringing to light the origins of the Japanese nation, and I was trying to describe the areas of Japan it doesn't mention. *The Holy Family* is a novel about the six prefectures that comprise the Tohoku region of northeast Japan. *The Holy Family* has those two brothers as main characters. While dozens of characters play main roles, those two are at the center.

An older brother and a younger. A family name that contains the character for "dog"; one has a first name with a cow, the other with a sheep. So many different scenes and events.

Now that dates have been introduced, I will continue to use them as I write. Two days before I started writing was April 9, a Saturday. Here's what happened that day. I went to the CD release party of a young friend and his band. He is the songwriter. The show was supposed to take place the previous month on the thirteenth; it had been rescheduled and I was going to Shibuya for the rescheduled show. The CD went on sale on March 16. The event space was packed; the fact that the release had been postponed seemed not to make any difference to anyone, or perhaps that is why it was packed. A great performance. Good energy in the place. Just what everyone wanted. To have music come back into everyday life like this, or perhaps to have an *everyday* in which music came back like this, is what everyone wanted. And my friends delivered a concert in tune with that desire. My friend, the leader, is also a singer. There was an encore. He took the stage again. "We had planned on performing this song even before the recent disasters." He continued, "We have been talking over and over about the song we are going to sing now, wondering if it is a good idea to perform this song or not, agonizing over it." They began the performance. The emotions were concentrated in my friend's body; you could see him shudder, could see the axis of existence, a staff of life, could see that his entire body and being was in the song.

"In this world," he began the song, "with twisted bodies, we're gonna keep running,"

Pelted by radioactive rain
We're gonna keep dancing
To the beat of this rain that does not stop
To the dance beat that does not stop
And again
Crank it up a notch

He had written this song some years ago now, a song that I was a big fan of from the first time I had heard it and now, standing in this club listening, it brought me to the verge of tears. April 9, around nine-thirty or ten p.m. Perhaps there are tears that don't fall as tears. I was crying. I was thinking about my next steps. The actual party was scheduled to follow the performance. Someone came up next to me and started talking. It was the rep from the CD company. He began by saying, "You know, this kid K," referring to my friend by name, "has been worried about whether to sing this song or not for the encore. He's been talking about it for days, was talking about it right up until performance time. I told him he should. But you know, Furukawa-san, he was so troubled because he knew you were going to be here today. K was worried about playing this song in your presence; he was worried about the appropriateness of singing this with you in the audience." I was surprised by this; I was surprised but responded anyway: "I am really glad he performed it." And further, "It was a song that needed to be performed; I'm so glad he did."

All my friends know that I am from Fukushima. I talked to K about all this later. I discussed it with the other band members, talked to other friends who were at the performance, had talked to other people I know. I had lots of friends in the audience, all of them young, ten years younger than me, fifteen years younger, some even younger than that. Over the years I have been involved in a wide variety of collaborations across the music, dance, and art fields. It seems to me that the intensity (or the potential—it's hard to put a name to it) of literature can be elevated by undertaking joint projects with artists who express themselves in different forms. Might simply be a way to expand readership. I want to deliver novels that are fresh. So with all these sorts of activities the number of "colleagues" seems to keep increasing. On that day, after two or three hours of drinking with everyone, I felt the growing presence of a certain truth, a certain reality: was I not, to these younger "colleagues," to these people I know, something of an older brother?

Someone came over to talk with me about love, about how to live after the disasters. My answers were sincere. Like always,

I am nothing if not sincere. Even if, as is so often the case, that marks me as an idiot.

There are two main characters in *The Holy Family* mega-novel, the older brother and the younger brother. It seems to me that I consistently projected myself onto the younger brother. I am the youngest of three brothers, after all. I was aware of this, and with that self-awareness I plowed forward with my writing (at least that was my intent). But maybe I have things mixed up. Do I really have none of the qualities of an older brother? Lucky for me that I am close to my nieces and nephews. They all call me Hideo-anchan—as in "older brother" rather than "uncle." That should count, right? They are all adults now, all in their twenties, but one of my nephews, back when he was three or four would say to me: "Hideo-anchan, when are you coming back to Kōriyama? Come back soon! Then we can play together again!" "Wow," I thought to myself, "I'm not just an 'older brother' but it's like I'm the 'eldest!'" It's like I am the eldest brother in some invisible family.

The name of the eldest brother who appears in *The Holy Family* is Gyūichirō, with those characters for "cow" and "first born." The family name is Inuzuka, with one character for dogs and one for burial mounds. A grave for dogs.

Another major aftershock; today's manuscript—a half a day's writing—goes into the trash. The Earthquake Early Warning system announced: "In the Hamadōri section of Fukushima Prefecture, strongest tremors at six-plus on the seismic intensity scale." I steeled myself. It was later reported that it was strongest in northern Ibaraki, a weak five on the scale. In Iwaki, four. But what does it mean to feel relieved at a time like that? A weak five is still pretty powerful. Do we really need to grow accustomed to this, and find no threat in anything lower than six? Hard to imagine.

For the past three days the hypocenter of practically all the tremors has been on the prefectural border of Fukushima and Ibaraki. Deep underground there.

Now that I've remembered, or become newly aware of the dates, if I am going to put them in, I might as well go the whole way. And if that is the case, I'm going to try a rewrite of that manuscript that I threw away. But I'm going to ignore the chronology. I'm going to work backward and work against the flow. I think there was a small event in Kyoto on Sunday, April 10. There was a charity event for the disaster, although no one was saying "for the disaster." I received information about it on April 1. Somebody had forwarded me the e-mail announcement because the original sender—the owner of a bookstore in Kyoto's Sakyo ward—didn't have my address. Three years earlier— that would be fall of 2008—there had been a release party for *The Holy Family* there. We had had dinner together. A young guy.

He said he had read a short piece that I had written and published in a guest column for the local *Kyoto Shinbun News*. He latched on to one of my phrases and decided to host an event. "Using imagination for good" was the phrase. Some of my comments had appeared in the *Kyoto Shinbun News* of March 16. The comments had been sent via the press agency. I wrote back directly to the bookshop owner. I wanted to express my thanks.

Moving back two Sundays before that April 10, to March 27, I participated in an event in Tokyo. The organizer wrote prose. My invitation to participate came from a poet and essayist who writes in a way that gets beyond the limits of "Japanese"; he's always writing in ways that push those boundaries. The event was scheduled for Tokyo, also in Shibuya, in a small club, the kind they call a "live spot." I was to read. Since the lineup was clearly organized around the poets, I chose one of my texts that could pass as poetry. I had to read in a voice, and from a text, that might reach the disaster area in Tohoku. But from what I had written in the past, what words would work in this situation? So, it seemed obvious, it could only be a section from *The Holy Family* (but it took two full days to come to that conclusion) I pulled out a section, something like a monologue, in Tohoku dialect. I thought I'd read it, but like a remix If I did this, though, there was no way I was going to read an episode including humans. So I chose an episode about horses. It was a tale I pulled from an area without a name in Iwate Prefecture where they used to abandon old horses. I chose the story of a now-dead mare, a horse with no name, from that area. This was Shōwa 21—that's 1946 in the Western calendar. Of course, 1946 is the year after the defeat in the war. So, a tale about a horse in Tohoku and *that* Japan—the Japanese nation-state. I was going to read, certainly try to read, of pain that transcended time and space. I was confident I could read in a way that would make it work. I trusted that the horse language was lodged somewhere within me.

The event had two parts.

My reading took place in the first half. I was backstage during intermission.

A girl came to talk to me. She had a copy of my book with her. She looked to me to be in her late teens; I checked with one of the assistants later who confirmed that she was a high-school student. She wanted me to sign her book, which I was happy to do. We exchanged a few words, "I'm from Sōma," she said. And then I understood: she was a refugee. That made her a refugee from the Pacific coast of Fukushima Prefecture, from the disaster area, from the coastal part, from Hamadōri. And, of course, in Sōma there are horses—the place name holds horses within it: *Sō* points to a long history, to physiognomy, and *ma* is the character for horse. There are, in fact, horses there. "I see." That was all I could get out at first. I tripped over my tongue again, but finally said, "I will go to Sōma." Which meant, "I want to see it."

Her response was immediate, "Please come and see for yourself."

This takes us back to two Sundays before March 27. On March 13 I received a writing request from the press agency. Now I was still fully wrapped up within the "spirited-away time," and even though dates and days had been hijacked, if I go back over it now I can get it in order enough to talk about it. I will lay it out carefully. This is now about forty hours after the monster tremors. And then an invitation came to write something, "a message for the victims" they wanted. I had been following the unfolding of events at the Fukushima Daiichi Nuclear Power Plant, but I didn't hesitate in response. I answered reflexively, immediately. "I'll write," I said. I had no idea that it would also be sent off to the *Kyoto Shinbun* newspaper.

One day before that, Saturday.

And the day before that, Friday.

I was in Kyoto. On March 11, 2011, I was in Kyoto; between two and three in the afternoon I was in Shimogyo ward, gathering materials. I had arrived in Kyoto the night before. That was in order to gather material for a novel. I had just published two long stories for the literary journal *Shinchō*, one called "Winter," the other called "Howling Wind and Surging Waves." I was in the process of completing another long work building off of those two pieces. I projected it at 240 pages. I intended to finish it at the beginning of August, perhaps on the fifth. That much had been decided. My plan was to get those three recently published, longish parts to work together and release them as a book. Title to be *Dogmother*. Its release date was nearly finalized.

The setting for the novel was Kyoto, limited to the center of Kyoto. During the last three years I probably had been to Kyoto twenty times to gather materials. And why Kyoto? Because the *historical* Japanese state is located there. A different Japan, one with capital-city kinds of elements, is located in Tokyo; for (the symbol of) a region that had been pushed out by Japan, as a nation with its own *particular history*, there is Tohoku. I had written about Tohoku in *The Holy Family*. I was always writing things about Tokyo. So I had to write about Kyoto in *Dogmother*. And, of course, the contents touch on the "originary documents" of Japan I mentioned before—the *Kojiki*. That's why I wrote the earlier novel *Godstar*, in which I have the Meiji emperor (or, at least, someone in possession of his memory) appear. *Dogmother* is therefore related to *Godstar*, not that that makes it exactly a sequel to it.

So, *Dogmother*. I had spent all my energy in 2011 and staked everything on *that*. So, if I couldn't produce something I was completely satisfied with, well, then I would have to chuck this novelist business out the window.

So that's the state I was in while in Kyoto on March 11. The fact is that this research trip was originally planned for two days later, on March 13. I was going to leave Tokyo late on that Sunday evening. But K, that young friend of mine, and the band that he was front man for, and their CD release party, which eventually ended up being moved to April 9, had been scheduled for the thirteenth—March 13—so I had already changed my plans and moved the trip back. I figured I would get back to Tokyo in time, no problem.

Even in Kyoto there was quite a bit of shaking.

Didn't know they had such *long ones* here in western Japan, I thought to myself. Which took me back to the great Hanshin earthquake of 1995. Tohoku never entered my mind, of course.

At five or so I was on the platform of the Kyoto Karasuma subway. I noticed people, then more people, with what looked like a newspaper extra in their hands, the headline leaping out at me. White letters on black background. "Tohoku," it read. "Deep in the Pacific Ocean. Magnitude 8.8. Numerous Large Tsunami."

Panic. I called my parents' house. Used a public phone. I got through. The next day I wouldn't have been able to get through. The magnitude was recalibrated at 9.0 two days later. In my hotel room I couldn't take my eyes from the television news. That's when that period of steady gazing began. That period relates directly to the "spirited-away time." Is tied right to it.

Now here is an odd connection (even though it took weeks for me to recall it): I was hearing tsunami warnings on that day, over and over again, in the live broadcasts streaming across the TV screen, but they were for Wakayama, for the coast near where I was in western Japan, not for Tohoku, yet everything, in those days, had melted into "Tohoku." Maybe this counts as the spirited-away space, too. And then, in that hotel room, it was the writer Nakagami Kenji that came to mind. Because of his Wakayama connection, on the Kii peninsula. But I had all but forgotten about that thought. Cleanly, completely. When I later started going over my thoughts, I had an "aha!" moment: When I went back to peruse the section on "Wakayama" in Nakagami's reportage book *Kishū* (that was just this morning, April 13), I came across the following passage and was rendered speechless. Nakagami was writing about the cholera outbreak that had started in Arida city back in 1977:

> One of the newspapers from Shingu, in the southern part of Wakayama, sent to me here in Tokyo, had an advertisement with the following statement printed in big letters: "No vegetables from within the prefecture used." At about this time I also heard about cars with Wakayama Prefecture license plates being turned away from drive-ins in neighboring prefectures. If someone was asked, "Where did you come from?" they wouldn't answer "Wakayama" but would give the name of another, neighboring, prefecture. We laugh at these stories now, but that's Japan—you never know where such outbreaks of panic will appear.

This morning, for this Wakayama Prefecture, I inserted a prefectural name that begins with "F." Most natural thing in the world.

"This morning" refers to April 13. But the "now" of the Kyoto hotel where I am refers to March 11.

So, think about a flammable liquid. A tank of liquefied petroleum explodes at an oil refinery and shoots off orange flames.
Numerous white-hot pillars of flame. How do you count pillars of flame? One "pillar," two "pillars"? Or, think about a
power outage that extends well beyond the powers of imagination. Reports say seven million homes affected. One can
only visualize it as complete blackness. Or, imagine flooded
airport runways, or think about bullet trains that have run off
their tracks. The bird's-eye-view images come streaming in one
after the other there on the screen. Or, imagine a tsunami that
floods water up into all the rivers. Then images from the coasts
that are broadcast over and over again. There are muddy brown
currents that by their height (and maybe by their sheer speed)
swallow up untold vehicles. Moving through there with quick
violence. Tail ends of cars being smacked around. Can't really
think of them as swimming. Or think of mudslides and how
many people, how many tens of people, are buried alive, not
clear how many people. Hundreds of people, no doubt. Thousands of people, washed away. Or think about building roofs
and all the people up there looking to be rescued. All this being
reported at ten thousand people. So think about night, a power
outage at night in the residential neighborhoods and the flames
are rising higher, this hellish inferno casts off an orange color
different from the flames of the liquid-petroleum refinery. The
petroleum refinery in Chiba Prefecture different from the
refinery in Miyagi Prefecture. Maybe it is Miyagi. The heavy oil

flows from the storage tank and is burning as it flows down the streets. So think of an earthquake that registers 6 on the scale, originating in Nagano Prefecture. Nagano? The news reports that it is not clear if they are aftershocks or not. So, another massive earthquake? I keep hearing this phrase, keeping seeing the phrase "unprecedented domestic something-something," over and over, on screens. There is a TV in the room. Even though the lights are surely on, it's dark. It's now way past midnight, so obviously we have started a new day on the calendar, but I sensed the beginning of the disappearance of dates. I must have been sleeping, but it didn't feel like it. I only get REM sleep; continual dreams. Even there, my focus is on the TV screen. And then I open my eyelids, and—no surprise—there's the screen again. It seems to me like the realm of the living. The *over there* on the television is the living realm, whereas I, I in particular, have passed over, on to the other side of the unreal. I am in no position to ask myself questions, but I ask myself anyway: why am I not among the victims? All of those people *over there* are swallowed by death, touched and caressed by the god of death, but me? How did I get off not dying? Guilt. To overdo the description, guilty conscience. Why is it that all those people *over there* had to be victims?

Days have begun disappearing, but it's morning. The next morning has arrived. The main Tokaidō bullet train has started operations again, back on track. I return to Tokyo. Tokyo had also been shaken. So, if I had been in Tokyo on March 11, at that time, as originally planned, I would be considering myself as one of the disaster victims. Would have been there for the tremors, a disaster victim, one of the affected. But I was in Kyoto. Kept back from *over there*. Nothing but the information on the television.

Am I really blameless in this? "State the reason you can live free of care."

The voice.

Then, concentric circles. At first, an order for everyone within a three-kilometer radius of the Fukushima Daiichi Nuclear Power Plant to evacuate; then, an order requiring everyone within a ten-kilometer radius to remain indoors. Before long the evacuation order was extended to ten kilometers. An evacuation order was also mandated for everyone within a ten-kilometer radius of Fukushima Daini Nuclear Power Plant; at the same time the evacuation zone was extended to twenty kilometers around Fukushima Daiichi. Two sets of concentric circles. In places they overlap. But, before long, a thirty-kilometer-radius circle was added circling Fukushima Daiichi inside which was required "internal refuge." This "big circle" looked like the corona around the sun. Around Daini was the "small circle." Subordinated by that "big circle," right at the core of the concentric circle, was the Fukushima Daiichi Power Plant, which then looked like the sun. Land of the Sun. The new country of Japan.

Those concentric circles would eventually distort into other shapes. By April 11 they'd already announced that the circles would be redrawn.

"But still," I thought to myself. This is long before April 11, while I remained wrapped up in "spirited-away time." What's with naming this whole thing after a nuclear power plant? Is there really any good reason to refer to the whole thing by the name of a prefecture that just happened to begin with "F"? This gave rise to concentric circles designed to deal with the radioactivity. While these two circles, the big one and the small one, vie with each other, they are actually collapsed into one big circle, which results in the second "Land of the Sun"; this newly born Japan pronounces this "Fukushima" to be its own. The entire world associates it with this place. It became clear to me again. Fukushima Prefecture was being locked down; no, let's be precise: it was being blockaded.

But that makes no sense. Fukushima Daiichi Power Plant is the property of Tokyo Electric Power Company. The plant is in Fukushima Prefecture so it should be under the jurisdiction of *Tohoku* Electric Company. Isn't it within the jurisdiction of the *Tohoku* electric company? Just makes no sense. And then I get these reports: one-third of Tokyo's electric power is supplied by Fukushima Prefecture. Or maybe it was that "one-third of Tokyo *Electric* Company's electricity" came from there. No need to track down the precise phrase here because this all makes the point of the situation clearer than the details. I mean, really. Circles and concentric circles. *Fukushima*—no matter how you spell it—was being locked out. People have been chased outside those circles, but it's all such an empty fiction. "Beyond the prefectural border?" Can one truly escape by leaving the prefecture?

I put my hand on those circles.

On the screen streaming the news.

I can feel the rings. They speak to me. "Go." I saw myself in the bathroom mirror, half of the hairs of my right eyebrow had disappeared; clearly I had been unconsciously plucking them. There I was, pale. "My god," I thought, "how stressed have I been? What day is it? What day of the week?" "Go." There was the voice. "You must go there. Inside the concentric circles."

What is this feeling?

All the people have been chased away. Towns have been abandoned. All the dogs and cats, and cows, and the horses, too. There is not even any effort made to dispose of the dead bodies. All abandoned.

I am compelled to stand in that place, but what is driving me to do this? When I analyze it I find that it was I who felt the need to expose myself to radiation, it was I alone exposing myself to this violence. I get that. It was a suicide wish, I am surprised that such an urge remains within me. I dealt with that in my twenties, but it had flickered out by twenty-seven or twenty-eight. By twenty-seven or twenty-eight I had decided on another thing. Can't say now what, exactly, but I can sketch it out. Self-pity is, in the end, the hatred of others and the world. So first, get rid of hatred. No more of this talk.

I know that such tendencies had negative ramifications for my chosen path of creator, of writer. Sometimes I feel this sense of "Why the hell was I born into this world?" Some of this is regret; some of this is an intuitive understanding of guilt and shame, overcoming self-pity. But I am not going to write about that, not going to search it out, and perhaps that stance is wrong. The wrong of ethically right or wrong. No, precisely because I have thoroughly pursued this already, I have excised the rawness that could be *mistaken for* the *real*. I will try to explain it in pseudo-theological terms. The guilty conscience that I mentioned earlier, I replaced it by strategically invoking the sense of transgression known as "original sin" in the Judeo-Christian tradition. From that starting point I used words and narrative and wove that sense into literature. I gambled on the efficacy of summary. Probably looks to the outsider like leaps in logic, or digressions. Since my understanding begins in the tradition of contemporary Japanese literature—one that was built on imported trends of Western literature, resulting in a naturalism that had ingested any number of misunderstandings that were, in turn, fed into the tradition of the "I-novel"—my digressions are the fruit of that vine. But then, where are the myths? Can one then simply deny the "creation" that is born of paraphrasing?

Now, given such a declaration, I must direct some questions to myself:

What of *The Holy Family*?

Why did I write a novel about the six prefectures of Tohoku, of northeast Japan?

And then, why such a novel that shuts in, blockades, those six prefectures?

I have always felt like an orphan. But why? It's not like I am one.

I was born inland in the Nakadōri section of Fukushima, not along the coast in Hamadōri, which is by the Pacific ocean; Hamadōri is now the central core of the concentric circles. Moreover, I was one of those who left town. Never had any intention of staying in the old home area. The way I remember it, that choice was already closed off in third or fourth grade. This "leaving" had nothing to do with affection or hatred. Just this feeling that that area—around Kōriyama, Fukushima Prefecture—didn't need me, had no use for me. That sense of things, and the present sense that Fukushima itself has been "snatched away," is, in some ways—no, in every way—different. Can anyone explain how, or the reasons why, the people that "remained" had to be polluted in this way? The voice again. "Go. Get yourself radiated." Or perhaps just, "Go. See." I was born in the central Nakadōri section of Fukushima Prefecture. Now I had to go to the ocean side, the Hamadōri, section.

But what can I do to share in their pain?

But I also understand this: I can't be too late, but neither can I be too early. Among the volunteers they need professionals. But I am no pro at journalism. They need volunteers who are pros at something, but I am no professional at anything. Nor do I have any of the nonprofessional qualities they need in volunteers. That's because I am the sort of person who distrusts good intentions that come wrapped up in too-neat stories. Nor am I a journalist. Well, then, what, exactly? A novelist.

A novelist unable to write novels. The deadline to start writing the 240 pages of the long section of *Dogmother* is pushing in on me, but dates don't feel real. Dates don't exist. A dogmother. I had not yet escaped the "spirited-away time." What would be the novel about the Tokyo Bay area that is the counterpart to *Dogmother*, the Kyoto novel? *Godstar*, that's what. A godstar. In that work I had the main character speaking about an earthquake that hit Tokyo Bay and turned the ground from that Edo-era landfill into liquid. Then, on March 11, 2011, it happened, and Tokyo Bay was liquefied.

The fact that I didn't have a driver's license may have been a good thing in the end (or so it seems now, on April 15). I did have a license for a 50cc motorbike that I had gotten when I was sixteen, but I had never renewed it. I had no interest in preserving that form of identification. This is also related to my "leaving." Not only was there no vehicle I could actually drive, I didn't have the skill for it, nor did I have what it takes to be a "paper driver," one of those people who hold a license but never drive. The trains were not yet running, and it was being reported that taxis and other hired vehicles were refusing to go into Fukushima. Further, there was no gasoline. Even in Tokyo the gas stations had begun to dry up, and it was not at all clear if any gas stations still existed up there. You had to know people up there to be sure of a supply of gasoline. So I couldn't go too soon. I had no right to act like one of the victims. Given all that, with whom, and where, could I talk this through?

I had at my disposal a number of ways to escape from within this constricting time. One of them was a manuscript for *SWITCH*, a magazine that was running one of my columns: I cranked out the twenty pages in one go and sent off the manuscript. The theme for that column was "Creativity (in novel writing)," which meant I could treat it as documentary. All the chaos within me, in the days following 3.11, could be written chaotically. In *that* non-novel manuscript all the urges could be laid out. All of the reader feedback to the various statements published while in that period of being constricted led me to a path of escape. Then there was another journal, the arts journal *Bijutsu techō*. A sample of the next issue, to go on sale on March 17, arrived almost as though intended to shake me out of the "spirited-away time." I had published a piece that I had produced in collaboration with a young artist. The work on this had been begun at the end of the previous year; at the beginning of March the artist checked that the colors looked right; all of *that* had been OK'd by the photographer working on it. So that magazine arrived. Something is being born, I thought to myself. A birth.

This project was not limited to the published article. Another novelist, Fukunaga Shin, was there at the beginning to get the thing off the ground, a great project that we kept expanding. There was an exhibit slated to open at a gallery on March 19. The preparations for the two-man show had been progressing nicely. But we decided to postpone it. It felt like an appropriate decision. But we couldn't cancel it completely. We had to re-create it. I realized this when the sample for *Bijutsu techō* arrived. We could manage a one-week postponement. That moved the opening reception to March 26. So we announced it, and with that the dates on the calendar—and a consciousness of dates in my brain—floated back into view.

In short, the artist and I engaged with each other to produce a public work of art; with a single canvas between us we went at it, brush to brush. For my part, I worked with a pencil, with letters and words, in the present moment. A little over an hour of intense concentration. When I looked up, the event space (a gallery in Kiyosumi Shirakawa) was packed, so full it seemed no oxygen was left in the room. I was deeply moved to realize that even having changed the date, and even scheduled at such a time, all these people had come to see us. And reporters even came to do stories on me, people from the newspapers. I was pleased at the way unadorned, straightforward words spewed out of me. I conversed with a number of acquaintances, friends, and readers of my works; I talked with some of the publishing people who had come out. But when I greeted one of the editors my expression was all business. I had already planned what I was going to hit him with.

I cut straight to it: "Thanks so much for coming today. But I have another thing I want to talk with you about."

With that S turned serious, too. He saw in my expression and tone, and the rapidity of response, that I was keyed up about this.

"I want to get into Fukushima. Over to the Hamadōri section of Fukushima. Will Shinchō Publishing underwrite this for me?"

"Sure will," he responded right back. "I will arrange it," he said. "And I want to go, too," he added.

He left the gallery right after that. I went back to my former relaxed state and continued the banter with any number of acquaintances, friends, and readers. We moved on to a bar for an after-party, nearly thirty people, I think, and I had a good time, felt fulfilled. Didn't get back home until late. I started up the computer and checked my mail. Less than three hours after talking with S at the gallery, there was a message from him reporting that Shinchō Publishing wanted to cooperate on this. I also had a message from Y, the editor of *Shinchō* arts journal. It was now late and time for another drink.

Technical conversations went back and forth after that: the fluid nature of the radioactivity levels, the risk of internal radiation, etc. In the end three people from Shinchō Publishing committed to traveling with me. I had to rethink things. I couldn't put other people in danger; I wouldn't do it.

"You still have to go. Go see for yourself."

Another scene.

An older brother and his younger brother. The two of them are in Iwaki City. Iwaki City is in the Hamadōri section of Fukushima, on the east side facing the Pacific Ocean. The novelist notes that authors of guidebooks, in their overblown style, call this "Fukushima's East Coast." That was my writing. The younger brother says to the older, "East is the ocean, right?" The older brother says to the younger, "East is ocean, south is Ibaraki." Younger brother comes back, "Ibaraki is in Kantō, not Tohoku, right?" And so they head north. Up Route 6, after switching from one stolen car to another. In that region Route 6 is called Rikuzen Beach Highway; older brother's got his hands on the steering wheel, younger brother is riding shotgun, humming, forever, "Strawberry Fields." The two are driving the car alongside the tracks of the JR Jōban train line.

JR Jōban line, the one that runs along the Pacific Coast.

These two brothers that appear in *The Holy Family*, the fact is that they also have a younger sister. There are three siblings. The younger sister watches her two brothers with their names that include *cow* and *sheep* move around Fukushima Prefecture; it looks to her like *sugoroku,* that chutes-and-ladders kind of game. From one village in the prefecture to another town, from one town to another village, on to some other hamlet. "Like pieces on a game board," she calls it. She asks: "Well, then, what is the end point of this game? What city, town, village? Where are they exactly?"

Sōma, that's where. Setting their sights on the boundary between Fukushima and Miyagi, they never got any farther north than that. They committed crimes, were surrounded by the police, searched. The two of them, especially the older brother, who was stuck with the "cow" name, carried a sense of guilt over being born, especially since this had led to the deaths of a number of people. Through hell screens, like on those big Buddhist renditions of Hell. So they couldn't be pardoned, couldn't run away. They needed a redemption. The two of them, the older brother and the younger brother.

This is in Sōma city. Which points to the last stop, the end of the game. The younger brother starts talking and we hear his muddy Tohoku accent. "Yep. Stop there. What's the name of this place? Sōma? Is this even a town? A city? Right: Sōma City. Yep. That convenience store there, that works. I'll get some milk. I need to pee, too. Deal? You're older: you go first." With that the younger brother allowed the older to escape. I am writing out that dialogue right now. Sort of a Fukushima accent arranged to sound like an accent of the entire northeast. I said nothing about the nuclear reactors.

When you open the big atlas to the page that has "Futaba," the town, written in big letters as the section heading, you find the following explanation in red: "Hamadōri is the Nuclear Ginza." Route 6 is there, the one known in that area as the Rikuzen Beach Highway, the JR Jōban train line runs there, and there are plans for a future extension of the Jōban express-way there. The first limestone caves that I ever went into when I was little (the biggest of the Abukuma caves) are there on the left hand side of that page. Over on the right side, on the Pacific Coast, is the Daini Nuclear Power Plant. Just a few *centimeters* above that is the Daiichi Plant. It doesn't say how many reactors are there.

We took off in the middle of the night. Four of us stuffed into a small car with a license plate from Kashiwa, in Chiba. A rental car. For the people from Shinchō Publishing this was just a continuation of the evening. But not for me. For me, follow-ing one or two hours of sleep, it was morning. So the ideas that come in the early morning hours and the kind of topics that get passed around in the middle of the night were all mixed together. Nonetheless, outside the window it was nighttime, clearly it was the middle of the night; inside the car the screen of the car navigation system was lit up. Up on the dashboard. This was no "spirited-away time," but there were time slippages. Time for us—the four of us—began to mix in a three-to-one ratio, and the days of the calendar, too, were beginning to slip. Ms. S was driving; in the passenger seat with an open map was another S—young S—while Y and I were gathered in the back seat. We left Tokyo and headed out on the highway. The route was entirely overland, and we eventually got on the Tohoku expressway. I didn't really expect the roads to be open all the way to Fukushima. Especially north of Saitama Prefecture, and up to the northern part of Fukushima. I was quite sure that for some time now all but emergency vehicles were being prevented from passing. But many places, wherever they could, had already returned to normal operations. We pulled into a service area somewhere in Tochigi Prefecture. Filled the car with gas. I was surprised when Ms. S told me that it looked like gasoline was going to be available when we got there. There was a cat at that service area. A female cat. A fat one. Y was petting it on the head. It felt to me that if the cat was fat the area must be safe. I had packed a bunch of fish sausages to feed to animals, along with other stuff, like cotton work gloves, rain ponchos, and liters of tap water that I had run through a water purifier and put into empty plastic bottles. In the lavatory at the service area were notices about the power outages scheduled to take place. But of course, all through the Kanto area there were these scheduled power outages. I saw how electric conservation reached into everything, darkened all sorts of areas, including these expressway facilities and service roads. I told myself not to get depressed about that. Eventually, dawn.

As this little car with a Kashiwa license was running down the highway it was bathed in day's first light, directly from the side, from the east. "There it is," I thought, "the sun is out." For me it was the second morning (second for *this day*). Next stop was the Abukuma service area. White breath in the air. 5:44 in the morning. Even with the slippage of days the hours were exact. Seemed to me just like the jetlag that follows an international flight. And seeing the white of our breath, it felt exactly like winter. "Just like an early daybreak in winter," I thought. But this was early April. "Beginning of the fiscal year." Stern note to self: can't be late.

Bright rays of light—shooting rays of the sun—bounced off of every surface of the service area, the metal surfaces of walls and pillars, the glass of the windows. Flying off at crazy angles.

Off at the edge of the parking area I discovered an old stele. It was a replica (had to be) of the ancient Shirakawa barrier gate, very impressively written: "From here, Michinoku." That brought a wry smile; at the same time, I was assailed by a strong sense of floating. Where are we? Where is this?

We had entered the Fukushima prefectural limits.

We were again speeding along the Tohoku Expressway. Seemed to be floating along, smoothly, like an object in flight. The car navigation system was set up to play radio frequencies as well, so we also listened to NHK radio at low volume. Mainly so that we wouldn't miss any emergency broadcasts. The morning news program began and, of course, started off with news on the current situation at the Daiichi Plant. We were listening to it on the radio as we continued north in the prefecture. Deeper into *Fukushima*. Then the NHK morning exercise program came on the air. An air of calm, the sense of comfort and familiarity, that comes from those familiar songs.

They were like those choruses we all learned in elementary school. Or maybe Japanese folk songs. Not sure what to call them. They brought tranquility even to *Fukushima*. Spreading tranquility, across the entire nation of Japan.

I looked closely at the roadside. We went past the major interchange at Sukagawa. My older sister and her family live in Sukagawa, on a strawberry farm. Thanks to her, I have three nieces. Then there was the rest area at Asaka. I looked hard. I concentrated on the scenery outside the window, and I was able to see the farm where I grew up. That farm was devoted to shiitake mushrooms so there were many greenhouses on the property. They made it easy to find. Plus, the Tohoku Expressway ran right next to it. Nothing had changed. A sigh of relief. I had been in regular phone contact with them since the phone circuits had been restored. My older brother—and by older brother I mean the eldest son of the family—lived there with his family, my niece and two nephews. I got an e-mail later from that niece saying "The hot water has finally been restored to Kōriyama." I thought of the concentric circles. This was in the fifty kilometer range, maybe sixty kilometers. I considered that arc. Since I have begun writing this, that being the thirteenth of April, the government banned transport of shiitake mushrooms grown in open fields from sixteen villages and towns in eastern Fukushima Prefecture. The grief weighs heavy on me.

After passing through Kōriyama we got off the highway at the west Fukushima interchange. That took us into the center of Fukushima city, right into the area of the prefectural government buildings. Then we picked up National Route 115, which for about four kilometers ran together with National Route 4. I was surprised when the Japan Racing Association Fukushima horse-racing course came into view, even though I knew one was there. We cut east. National Route 115 heads straight east. Toward the Pacific Ocean.

As we passed from the city center into the Fukushima suburbs I surveyed the landscape for surgical face masks. I wanted to see to what extent people were wearing such masks, and calculate in what ratios. The fact is that the concentric circles were useless. Actually measuring the amounts of radioactivity shows that these arced lines are ineffective: in the northwest part of the prefecture the levels were reported as "High" while it was also relatively high in Fukushima and Kōriyama, in the Nakadōri section, but that's outside the circles. I was trying to determine, consciously and unconsciously, what people do in response. So, among people walking along the roadway, and people on motorbikes, I saw no one with masks. Even among the official crossing guards outfitted with yellow flags and banners, none.

All showed bright and calm. What was I hoping for exactly? The guilty conscience again.

But then it was time for school to start. We began to see groups of kids on their way to school. They were wearing masks.

Radioactive material is most damaging to infants, children, and the young.

That's what we were hearing.

About the ingestion and inhalation of contaminated materials (what they call internal radiation exposure).

We began to see trucks on the road, more and more of them, with signs announcing that they were disaster-aid vehicles. Young S was driving. National Route 115, which crossed through the Abukuma Plain, was known in this region as Nakamura Highway. We also began to see middle-school students bicycling to school. One-third of them were without facemasks, which led me to feel a sense of normalcy. A strange trip. Feeling like brain overload. It was now a little past eight in the morning. A roadside sign advertised the well-known milk produced here. Made me think of cows and the *ushi* of my story. From there we entered the heart of Sōma City; this part of the city is known as Nakamura. That's the same Nakamura as the Nakamura Highway. The street lamps were designed with horse hooves and horses. Made me think of horses, and the *uma* of my story. In Sōma, with horses.

I had already decided we would stop at a convenience store. It was necessary for me. I had a duty and an obligation as the author of *The Holy Family*. That was where the story of those two brothers ended. But I passed up the shops in Sōma. We now turned onto Route 6. We were now there. The JR Jōban train line runs alongside the highway. We had arrived at the Pacific Coast. I told S to continue north out of the city to a place still within Sōma County, called Shinchimachi. Y was looking at the map. Shinchimachi is right on the border with Miyagi Prefecture. Fukushima Prefecture ends there.

We parked the car at a convenience store in Shinchimachi.

It was still early, too early to talk about overloaded brain circuits. It was beyond anything I had anticipated: they had many more items than I expected; everything available for purchase, as per usual. Cigarettes, for example: I had heard that in the disaster area that was one of the things in shortest supply. But there they were, on sale. And surgical facemasks, which I assumed would be hard to get as well, were not just *not* sold out, but they were stocked in multiple styles—and in large quantities, too. From the parking lot in front of the convenience store I—and the other three, too, of course—looked out at the sea. Even though the shoreline was still about three kilometers off, it seemed beyond sight. We could see what looked like the smokestack of a fuel-powered electrical plant, though. There in the parking lot we were bathed in what seemed like first summer light. A mere three hours after feeling like it was winter it now felt like the beginning of summer. Time seemed to vacillate. I was feeling that time had not yet adjusted back to normal. The sky was so blue it took my breath away. My shadow was sharply outlined on the ground, dark and black. The temperature was just over ten Celsius. Route 6 was busy with traffic, and the convenience store was filled with customers. All locals, I thought. I turned to the other three and said, "Let's go." Then, just a few minutes after leaving, there in our right-hand field of vision, on the east side of the road, like a surprise attack, appeared the terrible landscape of the tsunami's damage. Appeared? Perhaps; showed itself, for sure. And the scars of the massive earthquake. The map confirmed that a river was here; the tsunami probably followed the path of the river and surged inland. We turned right off of Route 6. We turned right at the intersection in front of Shinchimachi city hall. We felt, all of us, I am sure, our overloaded brains shutting down.

Just what had the tsunami destroyed?

This entire area had been submerged: It took days—some ten or more—until I understood that. When we arrived things had already been considerably cleaned up. At the very least, debris had been cleared away, and one lane of the road had been opened to traffic. But I didn't, nor did any of the four of us, see any bodies. Nor any recognizable body parts. We were overwhelmed by the sense of how powerful it was. The scene spread out before us, everything wiped clean away. Such power, to wipe out everything. There are no words for it. We didn't just feel it, we were pummeled by it. I am ashamed to admit it—I want to spit at myself in disgust—but I was looking at the scene as though it were a great spectacle. I thought of air raids. And atomic-bomb sites. It hit me like a smack to the side of the head: it's just like a city in wartime. I couldn't help it, I exploded: "This scale, it spreads too far." Said to people who weren't there. Maybe to gods and spirits. Cars that looked like they had been crumpled and thrown, vehicles lying on their sides, vehicles stuffed full of debris. We got out of our car with the Kashiwa license plate. We got out, walked, headed for the seashore. This was the eastern edge of Shinchimachi. It was also a fishing village. The asphalt ripped up in ribbons. Impossible-to-bend steel girders were twisted. We saw cross-sections of concrete. You should not be able to see, of course, cross-sections of concrete. Buildings of which only the steel skeletons remained. Were they really buildings? Hardly any structures. A helicopter flew overhead. I assume it was from the Coast Guard because some days later I heard reports of Coast Guard divers who were surveying the sea and the sea floor. Looking for missing persons. For bodies. Yet the flight was nearly soundless; the extensive scene carried an otherworldly stillness. There were salty breezes. From time to time the sounds of birds. Groups of two or three crows. Carrion crows. Some skylarks, too; their chirping was quiet. No gull-like birds though. We appeared to be on a beach. People used to swim there. A woman's handbag lay there. A hand mirror.

The sea was calm.

What can be asked?

Sand dances from the debris. It slowly becomes apparent that this debris is not just "debris" but a collection of parts from hundreds and thousands of other things. A house of which nothing remains except for the tiled walls of the bath; a house that is just barely such, of pillars and roof; or the house that is only a roof resting flat on the ground; a pile of roof tiles, strewn around heartlessly. We got back into the car and took off again, moving south within Shinchimachi. Stopping and getting out here and there. And then, there it was again. The JR Jōban train line. But the local train lines were all gone: only the torn ends of the lines remained; everything else had disappeared, had been destroyed.

A guardrail that abuts the railroad crossing is twisted every which way; it disorients vertical and horizontal, the direction all messed up, angrily distorted. A bright red metal box is lying on its side, a vending machine. Coca-Cola written on the side. Legible, but reading it holds no meaning. A white box of almost the same size, a refrigerator.

Next to the train line was a residential neighborhood, and an electrical substation was nearby as well; it, and any number of houses, had also been destroyed. A broken record lay on the ground; obviously, no sound to be heard from it. CDs scattered everywhere, mute as well. And a dozen or so golf clubs, looking like nothing more than bluish walking sticks. Uprooted plants and shrubs—roots and branches, all pulled out—withered. Or, if not withered, muddy brown in color. How far should I go in describing all these thousands, tens of thousands, of parts?

And this was just the beginning.

We made our way back to Sōma city. We pulled into a gas station. Were able to fill the car with gas.

We drove into the center of the city, then to Baryō Park, which includes the Nakamura Castle area and the Nakamura Shrine grounds. More than ten of the stone lanterns lining the main approach had toppled.

The shrine's torii gate comes into view. No surprise in that; I knew it was going to be there. No apparent damage. No torii were damaged. Rather than the usual lion-dogs, statues of sacred horses guarding the entrance. A single pair. I expected that, too. I had seen many horse statues like this up in the north, on the Tsugaru Peninsula in Aomori Prefecture. I had also seen lots in the shrine buildings over on the eastern side of Iwate Prefecture when I had visited them to gather material for *The Holy Family*.

What I didn't expect was the pony, off to the left-hand side, next to the statue of the "sacred horse of the shrine." By himself, brown and white, inside a small corral. Smaller than a Thoroughbred. Waiting, apparently, for someone. Somebody, anybody, anyone at all.

The giant earthquake had also destroyed stone bridges. So there were parts of the shrine grounds one couldn't get to. Ironic: these sacred precincts were now truly off-limits. Trucks for "transportation of race horses" were parked there. Which means horses had been brought to this area. I felt their presence anew. I nodded a goodbye to the pony and made my way to another area of the shrine grounds.

There were actually multiple shrines in the area. It was not clear which was the Sōma Shrine, which the Nakamura Shrine, which the Sōma Nakamura shrine. I couldn't tell. We climbed up the hill. There was a horse ground there, and a sign announcing it as the "horse pasture."

And so, ancient Sōma—the name seems to mean something like "reader of horse physiognomy"—includes the precincts that had been governed by the Sōma clan and is therefore broader than the area indicated by the cities, towns, and villages brought together under that name with regional restructuring; the area originally known as Sōma also encompasses the region that is well known for its Nomaoi horse-racing festival. The festival is jointly hosted by three shrines. Two of those shrines are in the towns formerly known as Haramachi and Odaka, which were among the towns and villages that were merged to make up Minami Sōma in 2006. The festival had received national designation (by the nation of Japan) as an "Important Intangible Folk Cultural Asset." So I knew I would find horses. I knew they would be here in this region.

Nonetheless, I didn't expect these sorts of horses: refugee horses, horses that had been driven out by the tsunami, injured horses. Some were in the pasture, some were in stables. The stables were being managed by an NPO. Young S had heard that volunteers were taking care of the horses. I realized only later that the horses being cared for here had been temporarily evacuated to a separate prefecture in a forced immigration, probably one step toward becoming permanent evacuees, outside Fukushima Prefecture. At that time I was not really listening to young S's explanations. I just couldn't. I was stroking the muzzle of a horse. The area between nose tip and eyes. The expansive horse pasture had been divided into two sections, one large and one small, with one horse in each. Both horses were thin. I first petted the horse in the small enclosure; he had lost almost all of the hair on one side.

Hair loss. Easy to deduce that this was a symptom of stress. From fear, I assume.

There was hair there on the tip of its muzzle. There was, of course, hair covering its body, and bangs, but also transparent hairs sticking out from its chin, like cat whiskers. Ten or so. I didn't know that horses had hair like that, like whiskers. The horse turned its attention to eating grass. Suddenly, completely engrossed. Its subsistence. I can't say definitively which kind of green grass it is. Seems like I should know; feels like an unforgivable oversight. All I can say is that it was "food." Sounds come from the horse's mouth in rhythm with its chewing, and the whiskers were all buried in its food.

The horse on the larger side of the pasture was looking at me. As the three others approached, he remained tight against the fence and stretched his head over the top toward us.

I assume he was frightened.

I looked down at his feet. I could see that he was not using all the available area. He stayed in one space, the area right near the entrance, the space, that is, where he could be petted, where he could be in contact with those who came to visit. Back and forth, endlessly, in the confined space no larger than two square meters, kicking the ground with his hooves.

I stroked the horse, but with no real idea of where, or how, I could stroke a horse in a way that might convey a sense of affection and care. I had seen the actions of riders congratulating their horses when they won a race, and I was trying something similar, but the result was meaningless failure. I could not impart even the smallest amount of comfort.

Those horses with bared front teeth, striking how big, and hard, are those teeth.

All this stuff: their taking in sea water, in the tsunami.

And still being rattled by the aftershocks rolling through.

No way to explain to them what's going on.

The impossibility, of everything.

The sense of numbness that remained in the palm of my hand.

The horses in the stables had painful-looking wounds. The stable happened to be empty of humans. Two cats were in residence, one of which was sleeping peacefully. Y had the other in his arms and was petting it. Photos hanging on the walls showed how closely the cats and the horses lived together. They told of how rich this shared life was, with cats on the backs of horses, shots of them as close friends. Y comforted the cat that would hopefully go on to comfort the horses. I hope they heal. I wish I had access to horse language.

Boom, a memory.

I recalled a horse now gone. On the farm where I grew up, I had found horse equipment in a shed that had been torn down more than thirty years before. All I had now was the memory of metal parts that had rusted on the horse equipment (the stuff I turned over, anyway). Horses had been on the farm long before my time. I am quite sure they were not riding horses but work-horses. When I showed up, no more horses.

Where, exactly, do they hold the Nomaoi festival of the Sōma area? Those festivals, designated as nationally "Important Intangible Folk Cultural Assets," were staged once a year in summer, complete with horse races, riders in full armor, and the battle of the banners. The festival grounds are over in the southern part of Minami Sōma, in Hibarigahara. All that territory fell within the biggest concentric circle, all within the thirty-kilometer radius of the core of Fukushima Daiichi Nuclear Power Plant. Within the area of internal refuge.

I wanted to explain to the horses that the radiation in the air is impossible to see, but it can't be done. No way to tell them, on this clear day, in the middle of the day, that there is invisible matter in the air sending out invisible particles, coming out of the sky right now. The light, being light, is invisible. Even on such a bright clear day. Precisely because it is such a bright clear day.

When the four of us turned to leave, the horses whinnied.

This morning (the morning of April 18), I started in on my thorough revisions of the manuscript, making major revisions to the earlier chapters. Had to be done. On the afternoon of April 17 the Tokyo Electric Power Company had released their "Construction Schedule to Contain the Fukushima Daiichi Nuclear Power Plant Accident." That was like another major aftershock. At the very least, they decreed, it would take six to nine months to contain the radioactivity, but further, they reported, the condition of the second reactor could not be determined.

If one starts talking about the center of a nuclear reactor, one is talking about the nucleus, about the core.

I start thinking about fiction. I remembered something I had read about Miyazawa Kenji that the philosopher Umehara Takeshi had touched on in his book *The Japanese Depths*. To trace the chain of associations that brought me to his book: The philosopher Umehara had been appointed to the government Reconstruction Planning Commission (Fukkō Kōsō Kaigi) and designated as a special advisor; almost immediately after assuming the position he voiced strong criticisms against the government proposals because their reconstruction plans left out radiation-related issues. Which prompted me to go back through his book again. But that train of associations is too complicated. The point is that I was thinking about fiction. And Umehara had written the following about *that* Kenji, the writer from the Tohoku region.

> He wrote many tales (*dōwa*) and poems, but he never wrote a novel. This is directly related to his understanding of the world. Novels are stories with humans at their center. Kenji did not accept that humans alone had any special rights in this world. Kenji took it as a given that birds and trees and grasses, wild animals and mountains and rivers, everything, had eternal life, same as humans. The world that Kenji describes in his poetry and tells of in his tales is one in which humans, even while endowed with eternal life, are fated to battle one another, but that also describes how to overcome that fate. I always considered that world view to be a Buddhist one, but it is probably a world view that already existed in Japan before the influx of Buddhism.

"But wait," I thought to myself. I have written novels with animals in them. With dogs, cats, birds, all sorts of animals taking main stage. Plus, some of the humans have animal names, the "dogs" of *inu* and the "cows" of *ushi*.

But that's not it either. There's a different issue. The current problem is that *I am not writing any novels*. I can't write.

April 17. Early in the morning I received an e-mail message from Y with a link to an online video. In his message he pointed out that the video had been shot close to the Fukushima Nuclear Power Plant and that we were quite likely in the very place. The uploaded video was titled "Special Report: Dogs and Cows in the Lawless Area of the Nuclear Evacuation Zone."

I hit play.

Inu and *ushi*; dogs and cows. They were there. Now what?

Had they had been let loose? Abandoned? Had they had banded together on the edge of survival, after all the humans had evacuated to other places? The humans having fled?

Even so, it is dogs and cows. Doesn't that comprise the name of the oldest brother?

Time to go back home. I can write only if I go back. The four of us got in the car, left Baryō Park again, putting distance between us and the horses in the pastures and stables. Another look at the streets of Sōma city. A makeshift camp for the Self-Defense Forces had been constructed. There were still scars from the earthquake. Maybe from the original quake, maybe from aftershocks. I wanted to go to a supermarket. Not some convenience store, but the supermarket that I think was the biggest in Sōma. I had heard that this chain, with many stores throughout Fukushima Prefecture, and with stores in Miyagi, Yamagata, Tochigi, and Ibaraki Prefectures as well, had been started with financing from some of the major national corporations. More to the point, the stores had started in my city, in Kōriyama. So whenever we talked about supermarkets, *that* was the one we meant. We parked our car with its Kashiwa license plates on the rooftop parking garage and headed into the store. First, down the stairs—the elevators weren't running. We passed a family on the stairs, headed the opposite direction; the kids were wearing surgical masks. I guess for kids it's like spring break. Actually, if schools had been open like in a normal year, this would have actually been spring break, but who knows. So even though it was lunchtime on a weekday, the store was pretty busy; it was not "packed" or anything, but neither did it feel like the middle of a crisis. Nothing to make one feel that way. We were looking to see how well the different shelves were stocked, checking the different sections, and while we were in no position to judge whether it was appropriate to call it well stocked or not, the shelves certainly didn't seem empty either. Yet there were definite holes: like the cases for local produce. Pictures of local farmers were proudly displayed, and the signs with write-ups about them were in abundance, but there was no *product*, none of their vegetables, zero, nada, not a stalk, not a bulb. The farms' addresses were almost all from Minami Sōma: still within that largest of concentric circles but still outside the twenty-kilometers radius. Minami Sōma is definitely *outside* that circle, right? The area that used to be Haramachi? There were other sections, here and there, empty of items. And while it seemed totally strange and unnatural, it didn't exactly take the "super" out of the "market," either. Nor did it seem to disrupt the equilibrium of the customers. But still, more than half of them were wearing masks, adults included, which was hard to miss, all the more because it now seemed to be a totally normal thing, yet, still, with all those *things* that were missing from the shelves, this *thing* just seemed so obvious. I may be overreacting. Maybe the masks are only for all the pollen that is in the air every spring. Possible, I guess, maybe.

But was Sōma always like this?

Not likely.

It seemed so calm. I turned to Ms. S: "It feels so calm around here."

"I know, like everyone is just taking things in stride," she said.

Surprise. Exactly right, I thought. "Calm" is not what this is. Something different from that. It is "taking it in stride." All one could do was be ready and waiting. *If there is nothing else to be done, what does one do?*

Then there was us. If the people who lived here were carrying on like normal, what choice did we have? We had planned on eating stuff we brought with us, in the car, but we changed that plan. Some of the restaurants and shops were open. In that case, let's support the local businesses. Leave our cash in the neighborhood. So we decided to eat food that they are famous for in Sōma, near the ocean, a dish of rice and clams. The Sakhalin surf clams used in it are harvested up north in Hokkaido;

we overheard this from one of the clerks explaining it to a local couple. They had asked where the clams had come from. We were at a place, a drive-in, really, out along Route 6. Tasted great, for sure. But we had headed about two kilometers south of Sōma city center, and that also felt different somehow. The atmosphere was different, just slightly. We were getting ever closer to the border. Three more kilometers is all.

I don't think that had anything to do with the concentric circles.

It is just crossing the city limits.

We set out again, and crossed over an invisible boundary. Heading south to Minami Sōma (that's what it means after all: "South Sōma"), a town that came into being in 2006 with rezoning. 2006 is Heisei 18. Which makes 2011 . . . I can never remember what year that is in Heisei, the imperial accounting. I have this deep resistance, a sense of opposition, to these imperial-reign names anyway. I had assumed that, driving down Route 6, we would run into a police checkpoint somewhere. We heard that there were none, but I had also heard that the prefectural police had been dispatched to enforce the twenty-kilometer blockade. Fukushima police; a blockade of roads. But surely that would only apply to the main arterial roads. Actually, we had just discussed among ourselves whether to cross into the thirty-kilometer area; we had given it careful consideration. I thought we should go as far as we could. It seemed like that might work. We gathered information. There were opposing opinions. Someone asked, "You sure we aren't getting desensitized?" in relation to what *might* happen, that is; I could see the point. Even so, I wasn't convinced. But I did think about it again later.

I mean, in the end, a "fly-by" is not enough.

This was not about it being difficult. Need to be vigilant. Time for facts: we had to check it out, go see it ourselves.

We only traveled south through Minami Sōma, through the Kashima ward, which used to be Kashima Town. We did some lateral east-west driving through the area. We wore masks the entire time we were in the car. We had each decided that we would put them on. Traffic on Route 6 was reported as being "heavy," in all the lanes heading south toward the meltdown as well as the lanes going in the opposite, northerly, direction. In that moment I found this surprising but shouldn't have: people from Minami Sōma would be on the roads in order to buy supplies, etc. Because, if you get to Sōma City, the stores would have stuff on the shelves. Nearly all of the drivers wore masks. You could tell that by looking. We then exited Route 6 and turned on to Prefectural Route 120. After about thirty kilometers, we were on the old Rikuzen Beach Highway, according to the map, that is. If we kept following Route 120 we would have ended up in Hibarigahara. That's the festival grounds where they stage the Sōma Nomaoi horse festival. The big stage for the sacred horse events, that is. This is clearly something very much on my mind.

We crossed the Mano River. Follow that ten kilometers to the west and you find yourself at Hayama Lake, stopped up by a dam, where you come into the town of Iitate. Three kilometers farther to the east and you find the Pacific Ocean, at a place called Karasuzaki Beach. I should note: you could tell where the beach used to be from what remained of the coast. The area around the Mano River contained many old *kōfun* burial mounds; it just had the feel of that sort of a place. More on that later.

We had now peeled off from the second of the prefectural highways. This was an area of rice paddies. All the fields were still in fallow winter state as far as the eye could see, dry and brown, but worst of all was the forecast that "depending on levels of radiation in the soil, planting may prove impossible" for all the fields within Fukushima Prefecture. What they call a "forecast," had already been pronounced, though. This from the government, no less.

The area was marshy. I assumed reservoirs for irrigation, but "marsh" seemed more precise than "holding pond." This because of how the surface of the water looked. The water, placid; the water, lit with an artificial green. Algae. No water birds.

Many water channels.

No hint of people. None. Zero. We got closer to the golf course that bore the name of that area; we may actually have been there already. We might have already come to the outer circumference of the concentric circles, we might be touching that thirty-kilometer arc, we might even be inside it. We got out of the car. Y and I got out of the car. Ms. S and young S were in the driver's seat and the passenger seat trying to figure out our exact location. There were all the water channels, and there was water running in some of them, of course, but for whatever reason our ears couldn't pick up the sound of the water. Cloudy skies. When had it gotten cloudy? We stepped down from the highway close to the farm road, stepped into the withered dry fields of stubble (dry because they had not been flooded with water from the channels). Fields upon fields. We walked. The crunch crunch of our boots. Y, being Y, set off in another direction. The springtime *fuki* plants were up. They looked good. By "looked good" I mean they were ready to be picked, ready to be eaten. And lots of them. I was trying to take pictures. But they wouldn't come into focus. Changed it over to macro-mode, still, nothing. Doing everything right, but useless.

I was sensing something; I let it go.

Eventually I knew what it was: not a single bird cry could be heard.

We had not seen any ghost towns, but we were looking at a ghost nature. We were in a soundless land; we were *there.*

I had experienced this feeling many years before. Up in the six prefectures of Tohoku, deep in that country. That, too, was a land with traces of ancient civilizations.

But there was more to it than that, here. Because an invisible light was falling here.

It was coming down. I did not remove my mask.

We needed to reset our senses to normal. We went back to the highway, went back to Prefectural Highway 120 (the old Rikuzen Beach Highway), and quickly got back on Route 6. We were back on the national highway, back to a convenience store. A convenience store in Minami Sōma. We parked our car with the Kashiwa license plates in the parking lot.

It was not silent but it felt like a silent space. There were buildings. In the convenience store not a single magazine was available for sale. None on the shelves. There were hardly any *bento* lunches, hardly any rice balls. Stock was sparse. Instant ramen included. Empty spaces on the shelves. Even though this was not within the thirty-kilometer radius "internal evacuation zone." Just because it was in Minami Sōma. Then there was the totally needless stuff. Given the dates and times, stuff rendered needless. Candy left over from White Day. A section that looked as though it had not been touched. Stuff that had been set out before March 11. On March 14—White Day, one month after Valentine's Day—all that stuff was rendered useless. Made needless by the date. No calendar dates here. Just like before.

The silence was palpable. It was heavy.

There was a community information board attached to the outside window, facing outward. A temporary thing.

The building seemed to be peace and tranquility itself. A convenience store. In Minami Sōma, in Kashima Ward.

I was standing there by the side of National Highway 6. At the intersection.

The sun was out again.

We headed for the ocean. The car was headed east. I thought it would be another two, maybe three kilometers, but appearing two kilometers before that was *that* landscape. The entire Atlantic coastline had been ravaged by the huge tsunami. But the southern expanse visible through the right-hand side window presaged the extreme violence we were to encounter if we kept going. Trucks from the Self Defense Forces: one parked here, then another. Self Defense Force troops: one here, then another. The wide plain just seemed dusty. But this flat plain, how did that come to be? How could it be this flat, I thought to myself; I amended the thought, for it was not simply flat. In my field of vision were markers that warped the apparent two-dimensional flatness. There was the string of telephone poles alongside the highway, standing straight and vertical, standing vertical, yes, standing vertical and straight, and then slightly aslant, and then farther aslant, and then leaning so far they faced the opposite direction. A section of electric line remained, but twisted. That's where the birds were gathered. Black. Carrion crows. An unusual number. Dozens of them; must be hundreds. They were everywhere. They went on forever. Another kilometer on, another hundred meters, not a single white seabird in sight. I checked the map again. There should be a shrine here, facing the sea. A Shinto shrine should be here, so there should also be a torii gate. Piles of debris had gathered to ward us off; the car could not go farther, so we four tumbled out of the car and started walking. Right before we had gotten out of the car we had seen a big, old, two-story traditional Japanese-style house. Apparently, even in this area right at the water's edge, things were intact, no need to worry about danger from the water. But when we turned away from the car to check it out, we found more than half of the first floor, save for some pillars and floor, was just gone. Like a slap to the face. The front side, which had taken on the full-force brunt of the tsunami, had been swallowed up by the wave, the wave that had been hungry for it. I felt a paucity of vocabulary; "tragedy" was the sole word that registered for me.

And what of the shrine?

Across the entire expanse, none visible.

Not a single torii. Not a single right pillar, not a left one. No standing structures. Nothing to be discovered within the field of vision. Maybe I had hoped to find the beautiful expanse of a shrine like Itsukushima Shrine, in the western part of the country. Despicable, such imaginings; this damned imagination of mine, that's what went through my mind. So, without surveying the expanse, I concentrated on what I could see nearby. I looked down. The sheer amount of debris, or maybe the way that it was *just there*, constricted my thinking. It was coming again, that shutting down of thought processes that I had felt before the brain overload. The way everything had been destroyed, the scars in all the various places, each one different at each point. So many accumulations along the Pacific coast of eastern Japan, *all the way from Aomori to Chiba*, and each different from the others; it came to me while talking to Y, while my words were tumbling out awkwardly. Finally, I understood it, however late in the game. But beyond that, what with the brain overload, things I may or may not have fully acknowledged within the memory: photo-like impressions and smells. Stench. Vinyl records were scattered across the surface of the ground here, too. Shattered. No two of them were the same, and each and every one had been damaged; that message was soundlessly conveyed. Private vehicles overturned, smashed; the accumulated violence conveyed differently in each one. Buildings reduced to steel skeletons; they remain, yet each one is clearly "not there." Motorcycles, crumpled like foil. It can only be described by using odd onomatopoeia—*gujari*. Caught in the debris was a large *koinobori* fish streamer; it was much too colorful. A farm tractor was crushed, upended, its paint also much too colorful. Its beauty, the brilliance, cruel. A large calculator. Hundreds of pages of documents. Some office exposed, turned inside-out. A round propane gas tank somehow standing at attention. Painted on the gray of the tank's surface was a cheerful character, the gas company's mascot. A typewriter. Also destroyed. No surprise in that. Someone had typed, pounded on this, but now, with this, no more typing, no more pounding, I thought. Even in the midst of this brain freeze I substitute words for the reality. With words. By words. I am a writer. And here we are, as writers, as editors, walking through the scene of the disaster, on the earth's surface, in the sand, we leave footprints. And that—as soon as we do, there is no way but to feel that that is a violation; no way but to feel that we are sullying things.

Then, after standing transfixed in front of two vending machines that had not been toppled by the tsunami (I was staring at the address written on its side; city, ward, street, number), after one slight step onto the plot of a half-destroyed house (and the small shrine that I assumed commemorated the family's clan god; it was undamaged), after looking over the swaying white lace curtains, the swaying hangers now without clothes to dry (had the wind been blowing on that day? Were there sea breezes?), after that, it was after that, that we returned to the car.

Had to wonder why they had not been crushed.

Today (April 20) I learn from the morning paper that preschools and elementary and middle schools in Fukushima, thirteen such schools in all, are required to hold all activities indoors. The Ministry of Education had informed the Fukushima Prefectural Board of Education that dosage limits had been exceeded. "Dose," of course, means a dose of radioactivity. This is not for the area within the twenty-kilometer radius around Fukushima Daiichi. This is only for the thirteen schools within the cities of

Fukushima, Kōriyama, and Date. Apparently the news came out yesterday, but I have overlooked real-time news. The Kōriyama Board of Education had already decreed that its eighty-six schools "should avoid outdoor activities." Did I really overlook the real-time news flow? Maybe not, maybe this was just not disseminated across the "entire country." The pace of news reporting continues to slow.

We set off again, leaving behind us that couple-hundred-meter stretch leading to the coast. Double-checking the map shows that there are many shrines in this vicinity. The map spread before us was at 1:55,000 scale. We also had the car navigation system, iPads, and iPhones. I had seen one of the shrines on the map identified as "Tenshōkōtaijin"—the name suggests an imperial shrine and points to the founding goddess Amaterasu— and had asked Ms. S and young S if we could check it out. I knew from experience that if we determined a target and set off without giving any consideration to local conditions or anything else we would find things we had never expected. And further, given that the shrine and torii located near the coastline were not to be found, I wanted even more to find one that was *still there*. Even so, with a name like *that*, I thought to myself. This "Tenshō" is the most elevated of gods—"Kōtaijin" being "highest imperial deity"—not just "imperial" but "Amaterasu," which, of course, brings to my mind that most ancient of records, the *Kojiki*. Now,

I don't think about the *Nihonshoki* (the equally ancient imperial collection of records). Why? Because as a historical document, that one is too structured; records that are *that* rationally systematized do not count as history, in my thinking. Why am I so stuck on this thing? It is Amaterasu who emerges as the central deity of the Takamagahara mythological heavenly plain, and it is the same Amaterasu who makes her appearance in the *Kojiki* and *Nihonshoki*. Amaterasu who is the first in the line of emperors, the sun goddess.

We left the prefectural highway and headed north. The wet paddy area was divided in two. On the right side of the car, the eastern side, that is, the fields were almost entirely submerged, ravaged by the tsunami, which is to say, by sea water, which had still not receded. I assume there is no real need to point it out, but there was no overlooking the salt damage. Indeed, breezes now ripple the surface and stir small waves; seems the area has turned into ocean. Maybe that turns this into the new coastline. *Now-dead rice fields* reflecting sunlight. I got out of the car. For a minute, maybe two, wanted to think things over. Not sure what, exactly. The water surface is like a mirror. Blue sky reflects off it, albeit slightly cloudy. The sun is going down into that mirror surface. The setting sun, the sun. The august imperial ancestral sun goddess.

Why death to the rice fields? Why death here, too?

We encountered members of the Self-Defense Forces. Behind them the disaster-relief trucks. We were ordered to avoid the area.

They guided us from impassable roads to passable ones, onto farm roads.

Then, the *Kojiki*. It seems to me that the role of the myriad gods, and the emperor, is to petition for an abundant harvest of the five grains, of which rice is the first among equals. I am not going so far as to reference the postwar symbolic emperor system, nor all that led up to it. Speaking personally, I find heroic qualities in the Meiji and Shōwa emperors. Nonetheless, I do, of course, reference the original ancient Yamato imperial court, and I reference the myths, the legends about a land that proceeded from the rising sun. Then what of a *Kojiki* phrase to "honor the land"? How does one sing praises to this national land? Especially now, given that there is a second sun in the nuclear core? A meltdown that has taken its name from Fukushima. Can a name be given to this particular sun deity?

Some of the shrines appear in the in-car navigation system and on our other maps, but many do not appear. In our to-and-fro meandering, looking for the site of the Tenshōkōtaijin, we realized the extent to which this was so. We found ourselves in front of truly meager structures, shrines not on any official ranking, not even rising to the official level of "village shrine." I assume they were there to honor the pioneers of that area. It must have taken much strength of will to settle this area. Many souls that now need placating. In one of those shrines, a big 1.8-liter sake bottle lies empty on its side. Somebody had paid their respects. The ruckus of a large celebration, the prayers for auspicious events. Finally, when we arrived at the shrine we were looking for, we found that the pair of big stone lanterns right behind the torii gate had collapsed into rubble. We climbed the stone steps, arrived at the second torii gate and the purification fountain to find that the area had been roped off, with a sign reading, "Danger, do not enter." The scars of a massive earthquake; sacred precincts to which entrance is forbidden. We were only there for a few minutes. The four of us then descended the stone steps. I took a photograph of the first gate, looking skyward from below the two crossbeams. The other three were already back in the parked car. I was the last into that small rental car with Kashiwa plates. Young S was already in the driver's seat with his hands on the wheel. Ms. S was in the passenger seat punching an address into the car navigation screen. Y was in the backseat. And there, tightly squeezed into that space where one expects the armrest, I saw him. I was the last one to get into the car.

It was him.

There is this command: "Write." OK. I will write this. I am writing: Inuzuka Gyūichirō was there. A fifth passenger. The fifth person in our party. "Write": The oldest brother of *The Holy Family*, the one with "dog" in the family name and "cow" in the given name, was in the car with us. But if I write *that*, I've got fiction, and this essay turns into a novel. But I have my integrity to preserve in this; there has not been a single fabrication in what I have written thus far. I may have been hesitant, but no fabrications. By making this essay a definitive "real account," I was hoping for something, for a definitive salvation. Am still hoping, in fact. I am aware that this is a kind of requiem. There are parameters to this. I had my own limits, which, in this case, was "that accumulation" of ninety-plus handwritten manuscript pages. Even so, even so . . . "Write."

Did I really not see this? Can I really say that I have not had the experience, the physical experience, of being able to see invisible things? Is that not part of who I am, pain-filled qualities though they may be? Has this not happened to me before, hearing things that other people cannot, being unable to hear things that others can? What about colors? I had already made public about half a year ago that I am disabled by partial colorblindness. I did not want that fact— it is a trivial fact, an affliction in no way comparable to full color blindness, slight even—to be brought to bear on things within the works that I had published in the past, so I hadn't said anything about it. But what I had come to write about had to do with invisible colors, imperceptible sounds, and ghostly letters. As a novelist I had written about illiterates, and, of course, of invisible worlds and invisible people. Why? In *The Holy Family* I had written of Inuzuka Gyūichirō as though he were a sum total of things. He is the oldest son, the eldest of the three siblings, and he was given the names of two varieties of animal, the dog and the cow; was he not living in an invisible world? And is it not true that I did not ever, not even once, deny that this is "entirely factual." His reality is not fabrication, nor is it the product of madness. Is it not because I keep piling up these denials that my work is not understood? But will not someone misunderstand? What is it with this whining? Have I not become aware that I am myself an older brother? OK, I know it's an unseen family, but I am still the eldest son. I have to have faith in the expansiveness of that family. I have to have faith in trust.

"Write!" It was definitely him.

"I have seen him." There, I put it in writing. He is there, in the back seat of the rental car, the fifth in our party. Inuzuka Gyūichirō, there in the car with us. This is how I start writing a novel. For example, with the sound of a voice saying, "Go there." And then, "Come here." Young S signaled that he was about to start driving. We took off. We were now leaving Minami Sōma's Kashima Ward. From thinking about the *Kojiki*, a chain of associations naturally led me to think about *The Holy Family*. I thought of all those poems by emperors about looking over the land, and, thinking more broadly than *waka* poetry, I was thinking simply of poetry, thinking maybe it was a masterpiece of poetry that I was after. I turned to Ms. S: "We never did see any *white* birds, did we? . . . There were no seagulls, we couldn't see them, could we?" I asked. Ms. S responded that there were no seagulls because, perhaps, there were no more fish. I was totally convinced by that response; then I said to him, in a Fukushima accent, "What're you doing here?" To which Inuzuka Gyūichirō responded, "Because I have chosen to continue forever as the eldest son." Then, augmented with dialect, "Ya see?"

Sounds more like that half-made-up language that was tweaked and inserted into *The Holy Family*.

So I asked, "Forever?"

"You don't know?"

"It's not like I don't know, but still."

Even as I was answering, I felt pretty sure that I was following him.

He grunted in agreement. "You see?" His composed tone brought me back to the realm of standard speech.

"In other words, you are to be the eternal firstborn," I said.

"Isn't that what I just said?" he shot back.

"When?"

"Now. Just a minute ago. So now what are you thinking? You trying to say that that's what you said? You trying to say that this was some pronouncement of yours, that I am some temporary construction you came up with?"

"Is that it?" I asked.

"If you continue with these stupid antics," he said, "you're going to lose your mind, you know."

I kept silent.

I think we had turned onto national Route 6. Heading away from Tokyo (by which is meant "heading north") along what everyone there calls the "Rikuzen Beach Highway," which is to say, crossing more of these invisible regional and city boundary lines, moving from Minami Sōma into Sōma City. The route might have been slightly different. I don't fully remember, but anyway, compared to that narrow farm road still torn up by the earthquake, this was smooth sailing down a well-kept major thoroughfare. It felt like we were flying. The sense of floating on air, to put it into words. The sense that this has already happened, the sense that this is someone else's experience.

He said, "I have nephews. What about you?"

"I have two."

"I have just one, I guess. My younger sister is pregnant, and in the sonogram you can see the baby in her womb, which looks to be a boy. But you can't exactly include an unborn nephew in the calculation, can you? So, I have just one nephew. But you have two, then?"

"From my older brother."

"Older brother?"

"That's right. Nieces and nephews: my older brother has three kids, and my older sister has three as well," I said.

"Three siblings," he said. "It's interesting how blood lines work. Lets you trace things."

"I guess," I responded. Three persons' worth of propagation; more precisely, the propagation of my three siblings, but I have no kids. So I change the subject. I want to avoid the topic. "Have you met him? How often?"

"Who?"

"Your nephew?"

"Just once."

"How old was he?"

"Must've been around five. Could've been three or four. No, would've been too developed for that. Must have been about five."

"Smart, was he?" I asked.

"Just like my little sister. No question about it. They look nothing alike, though." He drew it out slowly, exposing deep feelings. "It's really true. Looks absolutely nothing like the mother. And, you know, he looks a little too much like a cat. Like one of those big feral cats."

"More than the dogs, the *inu* of the Inuzuka family?"

That's when he explained that his nephew doesn't have that family name. I felt afloat, having spent these dusky hours in the too-smooth movement of the rental car, feeling like I was bobbing through the air. The "forever" of that phrase was a little too perfect here. Young S had his hands on the steering wheel.

He had described how his nephew looked. So I feel compelled to describe his features as well. I am duty-bound. I looked at the hands of this Inuzuka Gyūichirō who carried the dog (*inu*犬) in his family name, and a cow (*gyū* 牛) in his given name. But even before looking closely to observe, my line of vision was drawn of its own accord, given how much they had changed.

Just the slightest oddity in form, I guess. They were fighter's hands. I know from experience that if you hit someone, your hands swell up. Especially the knuckles of the index and middle fingers, if you get in solid hits (especially in the activity of continuous striking), from there to the back of the hand swells up greenish-purple, just for a day or two; it is proof of the rank amateur. But he had hands that had, *already*, been swollen and gnarled. I have seen hands like that before, in a certain strain of karate black belts. In fact, those guys have gnarled toenails as well, the result of their training. I will limit myself here to describing his, Gyūichirō's, hands. It was obvious just how hard the skin of those hands was. They had the odd appearance and color of hardened gelatin. The knuckles were swollen one to two centimeters more than usual; the second finger joints were also gnarled, from index finger to pinky, on both hands. And then the thumbs, which looked to be twice the size of normal thumbs. They had already been thoroughly toughened up, from extended drumming on hard objects. They call this buildup of calluses the "forging of iron skin."

They prepare this way because they fight in close combat, especially with bare hands. It takes five years, ten, fifteen. Takes more than that. Self-inflicted pain, self-torture of the muscle structure, of the bones, of the skin.

For example, human fingers: if you pack a barrel-sized vessel full of round, smooth stones—river stones are especially good for this, but small pebbles will work too—and then nearly every day you jam those fingers into it, a couple of things happen. First, the fingers turn into a sort of "instrument" and don't get jammed, and then they turn into a substitute that is almost as good as an instrument fashioned from steel. This allows pinpoint precision in striking, much more than a fist allows. A strike can go straight to the vital spots, all the weak spots of the human body (easy to imagine these: eyeballs or eye sockets, for example).

I am writing about strange things here. I am aware of this. I am talking here not just about martial arts but very particular physical skills, almost all of which are "military tactics." Right up there with sword training and spear tactics, antimodern tactics. But, even so, what I am trying to say is that, in a world different from our contemporary world it might have been sort of normal. I am about to touch on Japanese history. This is unbearably uncomfortable, to me anyway, all this history stuff.

Our history, the history of the Japanese, is nothing more than a history of killing people.

I am not sure of the best way to phrase things, given that rather inflammatory start. I will explain things as simply as I can. We live within the echoes of the Warring States period. For example, *bushō*, the term for military leaders, circulates as a commodity in contemporary society, and, thus, it continues to echo in everyday Japan. By the "Warring States period" I include the Azuchi Momoyama period right up to the beginning of the Edo period (1573–1603). I am not sure if the Azuchi Momoyama period is still taught as a single historical period in schools (elementary, middle, and up through high school). But I am quite sure that everyone learns that there was a period when Oda Nobunaga and then Toyotomi Hideyoshi ruled supreme. For example, we consume these two men as commodities all the time. When I say we "consume" them as commodities, I mean how we see them as "heroic" and think of them positively. Why would that be? These two were a rare form of military leader, which is also to say, on the other hand, and precisely because of that, that they were a rarely seen form of murderer. I can lay out details from the historical record. I will use both reign-era names and Western calendar dates. In the second year of Genki (1571) Nobunaga burned down the Enryakuji Temple compound outside Kyoto, murdering three to four thousand people. Among them women and children who had begged for mercy. Those very women and children were, *one by one*, beheaded. In the second year of Tenshō (1574), Nobunaga crushed the Ikkō-ikki uprising in Echizen. More than half of those that were confined by the siege were driven to starvation, and then, to give but one example, he built multiple fences around their compound to cut off all exits and then set fire to the entire thing, from all sides. More than twenty thousand people were burned to death. *He would not even consider their requests for surrender.* In the third year of Tenshō (1575), Nobunaga crushed the Ikkō-ikki uprising in Nagashima. He wrote of this in his own hand: "Nothing but corpses in the towns." This in a letter addressed to the military officer stationed in Kyoto.

He murdered thirty to forty thousand people.

That's the kind of man that that Oda Nobunaga was. How can we see him as heroic?

Given such figures, and to sum up those figures with none-too-fine a phrasing, one can see in Oda Nobunaga an "antipathy toward religion," and it is not hard to imagine that he found in the Buddhism of his time what amounted to an outdated system, a system of rigid factions that cohered around particular religious schools of thought. He intended to pulverize the entire thing. Thinking about it that way, I cannot claim lack of sympathy for his position. But even so, it is simply too gruesome. Still, there is an emotional part of me that sympathizes with him, tells me there is a richness and depth to this Oda Nobunaga. I find myself telling myself that I have to accept aspects that I do not want to accept; in some contexts, I need to restrain myself. Then what of Toyotomi Hideyoshi? Toward Toyotomi I feel none of the richness that I feel towards Nobunaga. More, I see in him a cold emptiness that horrifies me. A nothingness. Nothing there. Maybe just a meaningless, foolish, rare idiocy, an unbridled desire to possess. *And nothing more.* I feel I need to lay out, as simple data, his two military incursions into the Korean peninsula. The first would be the first year of Bunroku (1592), when Hideyoshi organized nine army units with 160,000 soldiers, although he dispatched only 150,000 of them. Then again, in the second year of Keichō (1597), he dispatched 140,000 soldiers. In total, that makes seven years of Korean invasion. Too many details: I cannot organize them into written form right now. I am much too incensed by these details; I just cannot organize them into written form. Nonetheless, since I wrote about *this very thing* in *The Holy Family*, I will quote from that. Hideyoshi initiated a sword hunt—confiscating all the weapons from every peasant in the land—and in so doing established the beginnings of a caste system that placed the samurai warriors in a class completely separate from the farming peasants; my writing continued after an explanation of that development. The author of that work, me, wrote the following:

> What did the samurai warriors do? Having unified this "Japanese" archipelago, they set off on an invasive war against the Yi Dynasty of Korea. They quickly ravaged the peninsula. Then this man said, he would go on to say, "Kill all of the Yi Koreans, render that peninsula desolate." Then he went on to say to his military generals, the daimyō, "As proof of your military prowess, slice the noses off the victims and have them sent back to our 'Japan.'" Instead of their heads, their noses. They were, in fact, shipped back. Preserved in salt, preserved in vinegar, packed in barrels, boxes, and casks, and loaded onto ships. In number, they

far exceeded 100,000. He personally commanded this. It was a standing order. Troops were sent to the Korean peninsula, after which they were ordered to gather Korean noses.

This man, this Toyotomi Hideyoshi.

Our ruler, under heaven.

There are parts I couldn't write. Those gathered noses are memorialized in a grave mound in front of a temple in the Higashiyama district of Kyoto. A nose grave mound. Mixed among those noses are those of noncombatants, of women and children. There are ears in there. All those ears, those noses, the quantity of them was to demonstrate military might. All of them, one by one, brutally chopped off. The supreme commander of this aggressive war was Toyotomi Hideyoshi. I don't know how anyone could be empathetic toward him. I certainly cannot. There is a vacuity within Hideyoshi; it is the result of his sterile hunger, his inferiority complex. If we look across the last century, which is to say, the twentieth century according to the Christian calendar, if we look across the history—the world history—of that period and try to search out a similar figure, everyone will say Adolf Hitler; there is no denying it. But *is it even possible* to make Hitler the object of heroic veneration in post–World War II Germany—the nation including both East and West Germany? Hideyoshi and Hitler share a great deal, such as the inferiority complex of the small man, and humble births. But to return to Hideyoshi and Japanese history: Toyotomi Hideyoshi enacted repressive measures against Christians as well, but his famous "antipathy toward religion" is nothing more than empty form. It is nothing more than a mania to grab territories (a detail of Hideyoshi, and of the Western world, that has been covered up). He was successful in establishing the foundations for the four-part caste system of Japanese society (warriors, farmers, craftsmen, merchants), but being, himself, of the farmer caste, likely the child of peasants, he tried to suppress all of this in his official biography. He left hints that he might be the bastard child of an emperor. Thus Hideyoshi consummates his nihilism in those evil, totally senseless campaigns during the Keichō era, the campaigns during the Bunroku era; he dirties his hands by sending across the sea first 150,000 men and then 140,000. And at that time, military horses were dispatched as well. Sent to the Korean peninsula, maybe thousands, perhaps hundreds of thousands, unknown numbers of horses. Lost to the annals of history, not a jot written about them, these horses. I only mentioned this historical fact in *The Holy Family*. Even though *I wrote it for the horses*.

There was so much anger when I wrote that.

But the horses: more of them later.

But to return to these provocative statements. Our history is nothing more than a history of killing people. What do you think of that? I am hoping it sounds more straightforward this time. If so, I can proceed without catchy summaries. Anyway, the real issues are ahead. When history is treated as "official national history," it is almost inevitable that you are going to get biases.

Our love of our own history produces in the collective populace the power to suppress, perhaps unconsciously—perhaps even consciously—inconvenient facts. This is not the intentional undertaking of a particular individual (or thing) but a covering up, accomplished almost automatically, via an anonymous filtering system. Official history is, by definition, a filtering system. All the more reason why these *bushō* military leaders are consumed to this extent. I wonder if I possess the skills to resist this. History that has the ability to jolt us: that is ideal—what I consider ideal—history.

Think of official history as a book. A book comes into view; it seems to suggest that it has no blank spaces, no margins. But it does, it contains blank spaces. In those spaces I cram my own notes, copious notes that are not yet articulated thoughts, and in the end weave a *new book* solely from the notes in the margins.

It's parallel history. That's the basic premise of *The Holy Family*. The only way I could achieve, as a novelist, a critique of that *official* history, outfitted with its filtering systems, was to work with the marginal histories, the suppressed histories. Or this: as a novelist I am able to insert some wild ideas into the assemblage and then call it a work of fiction. People will understand the paraphrasing of those wild ideas in story form, and they will be easily understood. In other words, I said, "Let your imagination run wild with that topic" to give birth to a tale. Good ideas sprout easily from a critical sensibility. Allow me to lay out that process, step by step.

Step A. As an example of this history of killing people, I consider Japan's Warring States period (of which some distillate still remains, still reverberates, still smolders as the source of so much even today). I start from there. I provide some abbreviated thoughts. About those innumerable *bushō* military types that occupied the Japanese archipelago. All of them rivals of all the others, all with their own fiefdoms, little countries, which rendered the country of "Japan" an agglomerate of nations. All would have had their own borders, but the majority were invisible. We can, of course, bracket off the rivers, coastlines, and major thoroughfares that mark borders. But what about the rest?

Step B. Mountains. I see mountains as representatives of invisible borders; they separate, are hard to cross. Which leads me to wonder, in that case, who (or what) crosses back and forth daily across those invisible borders? Simple: itinerant mountain ascetics. The Shugendō monks, known as *yamabushi*, the word written with two characters: one for mountain 山 and one that comprises the person radical and the character for *inu*, dog, 伏: *yamabushi*, 山伏. They are believers, practitioners, of a mountain-based religion, located on *official* Buddhism's farthest peripheries. Precisely speaking, the ascetic practice of the Kumano religion is known as the main mountain—Honzan—school, one of the denominations of esoteric Tendai Buddhist practice. Then there is the Yoshino ascetic practice known as the Tōzan—present mountain—school, one of the denominations of Shingon Buddhism. My personal interest is to extend the strain of religious thought way beyond the boundaries of this system of factional religion or denomination (which may be the essence of Japanese Buddhism) and identify the school farthest from the system: the third strain of asceticism known as Haguro practice. Where does one go to find the holy ground of that practice system? The Three Mountains of Dewa. That would be in present-day Yamagata Prefecture: Mt. Gassan, Mt. Yudono, and Mt. Haguro.

Step C. Which leads me to examine the connections between the celebrated *bushō* military-leader types and the mountain ascetics who are as good as anonymous. The Warring States military leaders, the *daimyō*, had countless fierce soldiers at their command, but the rank-and-file troops could rarely cross the borders separating states. One reason being that many of them were in fact farmers called to serve as soldiers. But if one cannot cross borders, then military activities, particularly intelligence gathering, are severely constricted. It was those mountain ascetics who took this on; I take this as established historical fact. Which leads to the following query: strictly observant Buddhist monks would have forsworn marriage, but what about those Shūgendō monks? Among them would have been some *yeisō*, who were the strictest in their observances. Probably a substantial number. Further, they were all "invisible soldiers" that were employed by the Warring States *daimyō*, and, naturally, they would have possessed military skills. Experts at sword, lance, or bow are too easy to spot, so what remains to a soldier if the obvious arts are unavailable? Body skills—martial arts—that's what's left. Out of necessity, the arts of hands and feet, surely. Extreme martial arts, which would have been effective during the Warring States period. That's what I am thinking about.

Step D. So I am examining the way these invisible martial arts, the combat of hands and feet, were handed down to successive generations. Obviously, monks who do not marry have no family lines, no succession of sons, to reveal knowledge to. It seems that there could have been only one way to pass on these arts, in secret. It would be through adopted sons. Sons that are not their natural offspring but serve as successors. But given the need for strict secrecy, a public adoption was not an option. It is my belief that they were kidnapped. I think this is what "spirited-away" was. Not hard to engage in some wild imaginings about the lineages of those kidnapped children: from the end of the Muromachi period into the present, the scions of those lines still exist, I imagine. And those wild imaginings get paraphrased as "fiction"; entirely appropriate, I think. Characters are born, and what follows are contemporary tragedies of murder.

That's as far as the process goes. From step A to D. This is the only way I could have developed the idea. In order to attack the "Japanese" history of murder that we have been saddled with I must create a murderer. Feels like a dead end; what do I do with that? Are these the skills needed for fiction, for creating, for fashioning?

But he is not simply something I made up.

Well, OK, those strange, deformed hands, I provided those.

But he has his own memories.

He is not made up, this Gyūichirō.

"I have this memory," he says.

I was sixteen. I wasn't driving yet. I would be soon, but not yet. But even so, "soon" was absolutely illegal. My means of transportation was limited to the bicycle. So that's what I rode. Always, always. Like, every day. Out through the woods, onto the forest road, until the marsh came into view. I would go across it, that marshy ground. Every day, always at the same time. It was training, so what you'd expect. I went as far as the charcoal maker's hut. Always on the bicycle. Everyone in the family knew it, the charcoal maker's hut in the mountain behind our house. I had no use for the actual hut. My use was outside, in the clearing. I kept a lookout for bamboo stalks cut to the appropriate length and width, and suitable grass and sticks. All for training purposes. I also prepared the wooden box. A box that I filled with pebbles I had dried. Sometimes I would pack in quite a number of round stones that I had picked up from the river bottom, to make a training apparatus for forging calluses. You know, right, that I mean forging my fingers? I am talking about my two hands, right and left, and the tips of my eight fingers, not counting the two thumbs, and turning those fingers into tools, into

lethal weapons. Takes years. Years and years, seems like. I heard
a sound. I was always hearing sounds. *Jarari* is the sound of the
river stones; if I thrust my fingers deep into them it sounds like
zaa, zazzaa, zaa. Hearing things not just when I was sixteen but
from years before.

But what I remember is one particular day when I was sixteen.
Not the normal everyday, but a particular day. I can tell you
what the day looked like; I can tell you what the sky looked like,
hawks flying high in the sky. Four of them, in circles. Four circles,
each different from the others, not drawing a single concentric
spiral. My younger sister was already born. This is the sister that
is now pregnant. My sister and I are nine years apart. Means she
would've been seven. An elementary-school student, with her
school backpack. I remember it as bright yellow. Yes, the color
of that backpack, I have a vivid clear memory of it, canary yellow. Given the time of day, she must have been on her way home
from school. It was a road through the forest that no one ever
traveled, so hardly a school-commuter route; I guess she decided
on her own to wander this road, aimlessly wandering around. I
think she might've been pretending to be a wild forest animal.
She just shows up where I was. Now, my sister never came home
from school in a group like the others. And for many years now
she has not said a word. No speech from the time she was four.
She must've decided to be combative, that she just "wouldn't
talk." And she didn't. Anyway, this was a day like no other. I am
remembering that day, truly unusual, when I was sixteen. Lift my

eyes and see four hawks tracing circles in the sky. Lower my eyes back down and see my little sister with her yellow backpack. She had come to the charcoal maker's hut and was now staring at me. Me there, forging my fingers, struggling to turn the eight fingers of my two hands into lethal weapons. Not a word, of course not. She then walked over a little closer, came over to where I was, still wordless; but of course.

She took my hand.

Took my left hand.

She stroked the palm of my hand, then she rubbed each of my fingers, in order.

"Hard," she said. To get that one word out took some tens of seconds. In order to say "hard" required the effort of her entire body. Took all of her small body. I thought the backpack might slide right off of her. I was stunned, unable to say anything at first. I was just so surprised, rendered speechless for a moment, and then was able to say something. I said something, it was something having to do with our being born into this world. Something, maybe something like, "The three of us, two broth ers and a sister, here, got ourselves born into this world."

There was a child. Until the appearance of a brother and then a sister, a single child, alone. Can't become an elder brother that way. Four years old, then five, then six. This is not the first of his memories, but he remembers the scene. Back there on the

Three Mountains of Dewa, he was spirited away. Having strayed off by himself, he could hear throughout the area, through the forest, across the space of the heavens, the ring of laughter, *KERAKERAKERA, KERAKERAKERAKERA*. He was not found until three days later. He was out there in the mountains, five years old, maybe six, maybe four, standing still, in a trance-like state. It was after that that the younger brother, then the younger sister, were born. So the child finally became an older brother. Indeed, became an eldest son. He knew that had he not been born first none of the others would have been born; there would have been no brothers and sisters. He knew, "I had fashioned something." Meaning he could not fail the younger brother and sister. Forever, unable to forsake them, forever to be an eldest son, cursed with it. But as he grew, he would see strange beings. He encountered the *karasu tengu*, the crow-billed goblin. Maybe a personality disorder? There was no escape for him. The fact was he was confined by those six prefectures in the northeast—Aomori and Akita and Iwate, Yamagata and Miyagi and Fukushima—and could not escape. Which of the memories should he believe? But the memories are there.

I have this memory.

I am talking with my younger brother: Really? You have to ask who John is? That's Yoko's husband. This John, he died long ago. It would have been the winter when I was three, when he was shot in New York City. So I have no memory of it. I never met the Beatles. They were not a rock band of my generation. But my encounter with them would have been when I was at the age you are now. During a high-school summer, during summer vacation, I first encountered the music of the Beatles. That was in Akita. I had stolen a station wagon. I had made a fake driver's license. I changed the license plate. And that car, it had this car stereo in it. This was still a time of cassette tapes. CDs were not that popular yet. The car could only play cassettes. And that's what they had, nothing but Beatles tapes. Tapes recorded off of vinyl records. With a handwritten song list on each one. I listened to them. Listening to them, me the high-school student, I took off into the mountains. I had a camping mess kit. I had rice, ready-to-heat curry pouches, cup ramen, a regular disaster-ready food stash. And I played all those songs. Windows wide open, played every last song. I really liked "Twist and Shout," "Eleanor Rigby," and "I Am the Walrus." And then I . . .

Nah. I'll leave that.

Young S was driving. Five of us in the car. This was no car being driven by a high-school student on his own, no stolen vehicle. An everything-in-order rental car. License plates from Kashiwa. No music from the speakers. A low hum from the radio in the background, thank god there were no emergency news bulletins.

From time to time I would listen more intently, trying not to be caught off guard. I was steeling myself, for if I was going to be startled, it would be on account of one of the nuclear reactors at Fukushima Daiichi Nuclear Power Plant, something to do with one of those reactor cores.

I had a camera in hand and was trying to capture it, the landscape out the window. Just wanted one picture that captured the movement out there, with no intentional focal point. But they all turned out too clean. I wondered where we were.

Had I just said that out loud? He responded: "A mountain, known as Ryōzen."

"Is there a town?"

"Just a mountain. A peak that soars more than 800 meters. You can think of it as a natural boundary between Date City and Sōma City."

"That name, Ryōzen: 'Sacred Mountain,' then. I assume there is a temple nearby."

"You asking about a place for esoteric Buddhist rites?" This time the question came from him. "The way you talk, sounds like that's what you're after."

"Maybe, perhaps . . ."

I had to think about this. Inuzuka Gyūichirō is now addressing me with an informal "you." Had I called him Gyūichirō?

"Yep, that's right, Gyūichirō," I said again.

"The Ryōzen temple is a phantom."

"How?"

"It was a mountain fortress. It served as a base for the ousted southern court. Fourteenth century. Then it was burned to the ground. Nothing left these days but foundation stones. No legacy beyond that. No documents. No official historical records, no history at all," he explained.

"But what about its being burned down?"

"You mean the historical record?" Gyūichirō, perhaps grinning now. "Third year of Jōwa, 1347 in the Western calendar. It's probably recorded somewhere. But 'Jōwa' is the reign name and first year of the rival Northern Dynasty. Wonder if it's OK to use their reign name. Sort of reveals ones politics."

"Of course, there would be two different reign names, two different first-year markers."

"Well, of course. Two strands from the outset."

"And emperors, always two of them?" I asked. But it wasn't him I was asking. It was a time of two different periods, strands, northern and southern courts, extending.

Gyūichirō's gaze was fixed out the window, off into the distance. To that far off distance; all consideration of me and my camera already forgotten.

"Looks like Date up ahead."

"Are we crossing out of the city? Are we leaving Sōma?"

"Nah," he responded. "Still a little way."

"Until we leave Sōma?" I asked.

At which point Gyūichirō said, "I had a younger brother. What about you?"

"None," I said.

Is that true? Immediate self-doubt. Maybe in an invisible family, I thought. And then the voice called to me again—"Hideo an-Chan! Older brother."

"Is it time for me to tell you about this?" Inuzuka Gyūichirō asked. "I think its time for a story," he continued.

"I'll tell you two stories," he said then. "One of them is my own very private retelling of the days following my brother's disappearance. It's unlikely to be very organized," he said to me. "Given how chaotic it will be, I don't expect that you will understand, but I really don't care," he continued. "But, first, there's one thing I need you to understand: my brother and I parted ways in Sōma. There at that convenience store in Sōma. Maybe you know about that already. You may already be aware of the scene at the convenience store where the paths of our lives separated for good.

"Not that it really matters one way or the other."

My brother allowed me to get away. In a way, he left me *outside of time*. Whether it was outside time, or the story, or whatever, the details are not important. But you, this is something you need to think about: if I had been able to escape *outside the story*, then it makes perfect sense that I am here now.

By here, I mean right here beside you, right now, in the cramped back seat of this car. Right now—what year is it anyway?

2011, April?

April 5? 6?

That's the Western calendar, right? What year is that in the imperial-reign system?

Heisei 23.

So Heisei has really come a long way. I was born in Shōwa 52, year of my birth. But I only made it as far as Heisei 15, there, *inside of time, inside the story,* until the I met the conclusion at that convenience store in Sōma.

That's where I lost track of my brother.

I told you I was going to give you my private version of all of that, about those days following my brother's disappearance, but it's pointless. Here's the thing, "days" don't exist, you see. You know what I mean? Because I moved outside of time. There at that convenience store, at the point where my brother allowed me to escape time.

And with that, history felt closer.

Maybe because time no longer "exists." Maybe because all of history has come to seem like something compressed, like it's contained in a swimming pool. But that's not it, that example doesn't work either. Because, you know, it's like I'm able to dive into its depths. That's how it feels, in fact; this sense that time does *not* exist while history *does.*

OK, OK—looks like I'll be scolded if I continue being this careless about history.

Even so, I am going to borrow some of what you know and tell the second of my stories. Forget about my own story for awhile. Way too jumbled. Now this second story, that, of course, is about horses.

It's an association one can make from the name of the place, from Sōma, am I right?

And you have already written about this, haven't you: "There are horses in the city of Sōma." Of course there are, it's right in the name of the place. So of course they're there.

So, let's move on and talk about horses.

"Let me tell you about horses," he said to me. "You're not going to say, 'Enough of horses already, I've heard enough,' or something else like that, are you? Before getting into the actual story of the horses, maybe I should provide a summary, an outline of horses. We all know horses are domestic livestock; obvious, right? But then, what does that mean?"

" 'Domestic livestock' are obviously special animals, right?"

Birds and beasts that are raised and cared for by humans.

Now, to be precise, to limit ourselves to "birds and beasts," would be to make a mistake: silkworms are insects and goldfish are fish, but they have also been domesticated. But let's not be concerned with such details. There are the "five domestic animals" comprising fowl, sheep, cattle, horses, and pigs; there is a group of "six domestic animals" that includes dogs. That broadbrush approach will work for us, right?

Well, then, within this group of "five domestic animals" or the "group of six," what is consistent across all of these "special animals"?

Just saying they are raised by humans won't cut it. Captured from the wild, raised and acclimated, made domestic: that might make the birds and beasts into pets, but into domestic breeds?

No, that's not it. That would not be sufficient for them to develop into breeds.

Those breeds were devised by humans; that is the essential point. Beyond that there is nothing.

How about a different expression: "natural selection." All living beasts are naturally weeded out. Some get to go on living, some do not. That's what happens. But domestic animals have been naturally selected by humans. Whether a particular variety dies out or flourishes is dependent on the contribution of humans.

It's a contract, you see.

The animals that have entered into a contract with the humans are the ones that become domestic animals.

In the Judeo-Christian tradition we humans have entered into a contract with God, and all the domestic animals have been bequeathed to our care. Even if we acknowledge that all living beings have been given life by God, we cannot overlook the fact that, after that, we've entered a contract with the animals. Fact is, on account of that, we are now controlling them, whether five varieties or six varieties or however many dozens of varieties of living beings there are.

So we are the administrators of giving birth and of being born. That's domestication; that's the contract.

We humans continue orchestrating this natural selection, at least to the degree that we continue to raise domestic animals. That's the contract, continually renewed, between us and the domestic animals.

You disagree with any of this?

I didn't think so.

From this point on I will divide "domestic livestock" into two groups. It makes things easier that way. Now, why is it that humans needed *new breeds* of domestic animals? Because one group was for eating and one group was for working. From that list of five varieties, chickens were in the former group. For meat and also for eggs. Sheep were also in the former category, with the added advantage of providing wool. In Japan, cattle were in the latter category. In the fields, they pulled plows; in the cities they were kept in order to provide an engine for carriages. As for meat eating, the idea of using them as a source of animal-based protein, that idea didn't exist in the public sphere until we started *imitating* Western civilization in the nineteenth century. Milk was an exception, from the outset, cow's milk and the products made from it placed them in the former group. Leather, too.

But what about horses?

Horses were in the latter category.

Of course, they served a role similar to that of cows. Useful for farming the land. More technically, to draw loads, as draft horses. The thing that stands out for horses, of course, when compared to cattle, is their ability to be ridden. This has no comparison to cattle, which can only be used as the engines to move carriages; horses are the source of energy, but they are also the conveyance.

A horse's value is derived from its being "rideable livestock."

But horses have also served as an engine of *world* history.

Horses were a driving force of world history, which, of course, encompasses Japanese history, as well.

Goes without saying. I'm sure you agree.

And war, too: horses changed the structure of war, both ethnic conflict and state-waged war. We can assume that war existed even before horses; there were wars all throughout the ancient world, but with the appearance of this "rideable livestock," the nature of war changed dramatically. You can imagine how this worked in the early stages. There were groups and nations that understood horses, that made use of horses, and these "horse-advanced nations" appear in the historical record as victorious in battle and go on to become conquerors. Easy enough to imagine the story line. Horses provided unparalleled military power. They would have been the ultimate weapon in prehistory and, indeed, continued to be so until the advent of firearms. With their speed, the pace of attack changes; it brought an unbelievable maneuverability, especially when bows, which could be employed from horseback, were added to the mix.

Of course, this is only at the earliest stages; before long, all parties involved with war came to understand horses and to use them.

In any case, the very structure of war was changed.

As a result, world history, human history, can be divided into a "before horses" and an "after horses."

To the extent of my own knowledge, the oldest traces of horses' being domesticated are in southern Ukraine. Teeth have been found among the artifacts from the Neolithic period. Horse teeth. Carbon-14 dating estimates that the artifacts and the sites are about 5,000 years old, and probably 500 years older than that.

Of course, the ancient Egyptians had horses too.

They were also in the Assyrian city-state.

And also in Greece and Rome.

But what were horses to these civilizations? Different from cattle, different from sheep and fowl. Unlike pigs and dogs. These rideable domestic animals, tightly associated at a basic level with war, were, in most civilized societies, the possession of the ruling classes, which is to say, a symbol of ruling and governing. Things were no different in Japan. In the early years after the institution of twelfth-century legal codes, we see the same scenario, namely, the samurai warrior class as rulers in possession of horses.

Horses and samurai. The image just sort of presents itself, don't you think?

But if we are talking about horses in Japan, there are historical vicissitudes. Allow me to explain. There were initially three varieties of horses, all of which have risen and fallen, by turns. That's too general but still accurate. The three varieties are separated according to size. Small and medium-sized horses, along with the large horses. Now it was not until Japan ended its policy of seclusion that this third variety entered our history. But ever since the Meiji period, and even now, what comes to mind as the standard, stereotypical "horse" is only this third variety. Big as Thoroughbreds, standing as high as 170 centimeters.

The medium-sized horses stand about 130 centimeters.

And the small ones don't quite reach 120 centimeters.

You can imagine what they must look like. Quite cute, don't you think?

They were the very first Japanese horse. The original breed was a horse small in stature. I mean, this is not entirely conclusive. Horse bones have been dug up among Jōmon-period items, so it had long been accepted that there were horses at that time. But scientific measurements of fluoride isotopes overturned that accepted wisdom. A newer explanation is gaining acceptance that no horses were in Japan until the start of the Kofun period, in the early third century. During the Kofun period, which followed the Jōmon and Yayoi periods, it was the medium-sized horses that arrived in Japan; no one disagrees with this. To suggest another theory, it seems likely that one of those "horse-advanced nations" invaded the Japanese archipelago. And that makes it seem likely that present day "Japan" was developed by this same ethnic group or nation-state that already understood, and was raising, horses. I imagine this makes you think of sections in the *Kojiki*, the *Record of Ancient Matters* that explains Japan's origins. Am I right? About the arrival of the emperor to Japan.

But that, my friend, is *not the official history*.

So, suppose that the small horses—ponies—were already "here" during the Jōmon and Yayoi periods. And suppose as well that a culture of horse husbandry was already established in the prehistoric period. And further, the end of that line of small-sized horses remains, as a contemporary breed. They are on the Nansei Islands. A very few head remain in the Yaeyama Islands, in Yonaguni, and in the Tokara Islands, which is Okinawa and Kagoshima Prefectures, according to current geographic delineations. I bet you're thinking that forcing this into contemporary geographic divisions is a bit heavy-handed. Am I right? Thinking: "Were the Nansei Islands territorial possessions of 'Japan' at that time?"

And then, as you start thinking about the word *nansei*—south and west—of the Nansei Islands it leads you to an association with the north and east of Tohoku.

The opposite of Nansei would be Tohoku; southwest and northeast.

And that, I bet, leads you back to associations with the *Kojiki*. There, Japan's main island, Honshū, is given the name "Ōyamato Toyoakizushima," and the story is told of the island's founding. But, in fact, that island was understood to refer only to the *kinai* imperial holdings near Kyoto, so Tohoku was not included in that story. In other words, from the very beginning, the northeastern prefectures of Tohoku were *not even considered part of Honshū*. I am sure that this has been on your mind as well. And I assume with those peculiar scales of yours you are calculating the fortune and misfortune that followed from being excluded from those founding myths.

At any rate, we only know three things for sure. In the land currently occupied by the nation-state of Japan, there are three varieties of horses. Of those, the small and mid-sized horses, the ones that can be considered among the original horses, are in danger of extinction. Whenever we think of "horses," the image we have of a "horse" is, without fail, even within Japan, always of those large horses.

There is an easy-to-understand chart compiled in the Meiji period that plots those changes. I will use it to explain this. It says that horses are to be divided into the three following categories: "Japanese breeds," "mixed breeds," and "Western breeds." That third category, the Western breeds, refers to a big horse that simply *did not exist* before the opening of Japan in the late 1800s. They were imported, imported in waves. Which led to mixed breeds and produced the horse breeds of the second category.

The mixed breeds were promoted by the Meiji government. Horses were wanted for military purposes, and military horses had to be big and strong. Also, Japan felt it had to develop as a "rich nation, strong army." And then the horses themselves needed improving, improvement of the breed. And with that, they transformed from "Japanese breeds" to "mixed breeds." It is not impossible that in the final step they transformed into actual "Western breeds." Artificial selection allows the creation of a variety, a "domesticated animal."

And, in fact, they accomplished this transformation.

Am I right? The original horses no longer exist.

Unless you go looking for them; you have to really look to find them.

You see how Japanese history was commanding the "Japanese breeds" to disappear? Now, it's not accurate to say that all the descendants died out. Descendants still exist, whether in large numbers or small. And that fact has a direct relationship to the horses of Sōma, to the story I am about to tell. The story of the horses of the Sōma clan and of Sōma City.

But before I get into that, I have one more story to tell. I have to tell this story in a way that you will not be able to forget or in a way that none of us will be misled. You ready for this? All those historical dramas that claim to be factual? Don't believe 'em. All those grand battle scenes from the movies, those dramas with the *bushō* military leaders? Don't believe a word.

Nothing but lies.

The horses that appear in them are all wrong.

You know why, right? Those big horses didn't exist back then. Nonetheless, all the samurai we see in the movies are saddled to the backs of Thoroughbred race horses, or regular

Thoroughbreds, and sent out into the battlefield.

The scale of those horses? Fabrication, total fabrication. Entirely made up. And with all that, there is not a single *consumer* to be found who thinks otherwise.

So, let's move to stories about the horses of Sōma. There are actually two stories here, but I sense that they are going to flow together into a single tale. One of those stories is, obviously, my story. The tale in which I cross outside of time.

Those were his words to me: "Let me tell a story of Sōma horses. To do so, I must tell you about the Sōma clan's founding patriarch, who became the head of the Sōma clan and domains during the Edo period. Now, don't come back to me with any of that 'Sōma domain? I don't get that' stuff. Whatever; it is essential to get hold of a summary, an outline of the Sōma clan. OK with you if I provide a simple overview?"

He continued: The Sōma clan was one of the most solidly established old families of "Japan."

In fact, the Sōma clan had administered the same stretch of land in the Hamadōri section of Fukushima from the Kamakura period right up to the fourth year of Meiji, which, calculated by the Western calendar, stretches from the twelfth century up to 1871. An unbroken rule. They suffered none of the territorial shakeups meted out by the *bakufu* government. This is extremely rare in the annals of Japanese history. They lasted right up until 1871, when the fiefs were abolished and the prefectures established.

For nearly 700 years the Sōma clan were *based in* Sōma.

Before that they were in Shimousa. That's Chiba Prefecture on a contemporary map. The Sōma clan constituted one of the main branches of the Kantō-based Chiba clan. In 1323 by the Western calendar—Genkō 3 (元亨 3)—they moved their base of operations to Ōshū, which constituted most of contemporary Tohoku. That's the usual story. Another version has them moving in Genkō 3 (元弘 3)—same sound but a different reign name. That would be 1333.

And that's the year that the Kamakura *bakufu* government collapsed.

But what matters more than reign name or era, which is to say, more than the time frame, is the space—from the horses' perspective, I mean. What matters is less the 1323 or 1333 than the migration from the aforementioned Chiba to Fukushima. For the horses of the Sōma clan, this is the big migration. These were military horses. The symbol of the samurai.

So there was a huge migration.

And then the horses were, from time to time, dispatched on military activities. There was Ashikaga Takauji, who raised an army, which the Sōma clan joined forces with, to do battle with Kitabatake Akiie, who was the commander of defense for the Mutsu domain. And this Ashikaga Takauji, he was the one who became the first shōgun of the Muromachi *bakufu*. That's when Japanese history encounters the turmoil of the Nanboku era, the split of the North and South Dynasties. Which is when "Japan" gets embroiled in, is engrossed in, disturbances and upheavals. And that's when the daimyō of the Warring States period appear.

And the Sōma clan was among them.

So from time to time they were dispatched on military activities. Actually, let's proceed from the horses' point of view. In the fifty years starting from 1540—in reign names, that is, from Tenbun 5 until Tenshō 18—there were movements and military excursions but none that qualify as a migration. At any rate, the long-standing foe of the Sōma was the Date clan, right next door. In that fifty-year period they engaged in battle a total of thirty times. The horses undertook numerous short trips to the borders of the clan lands, sometimes midrange trips, and then battle.

These were real battles, on a grand scale.

And then, death on the battlefield, or if not death then a return to produce offspring, or even if not dead but at times weaving through the battlefield with the corpses of the fallen "riders" still on their backs. The back-and-forth of these battles are etched in their memories.

Awful memories. These don't disappear in a single generation; erasure is impossible.

Then in Tenshō 18, which is 1590 in the Western calendar, following a substantial passage of time, another migration. This time, Date Masamune, the leader of what had been the long-standing enemy clan, is now an ally. And together they joined Toyotomi Hideyoshi's famous siege of Odawara Castle. The Sōma horses were all dispatched from Fukushima Prefecture to distant Kanagawa Prefecture. Some of them died there; some of them remained to live on in that region, with all of these awful experiences etched into their memories. Now, they were not dispatched all the way to the decisive battle at Sekigahara. They did not make the long migration to Sekigahara, in what is now Gifu Prefecture, in Keichō 5, which is 1600, and that earned them the displeasure of Tokugawa Ieyasu and brought substantial grief. To the Sōma leader, that is. But somehow or other the Sōma fief was established, and then Osaka Castle fell, which meant the downfall of the Toyotomi dynasty and the rise to power of the Tokugawa, and from that point on the horses *were in Sōma*.

They were in the Sōma region, under the jurisdiction of the Sōma clan.

They did not deploy. There were no deployments.

Three more things I want to add. Throughout all of this the Sōma clan continued the religious festival that is the Nomaoi. This is the festival that is now designated, by the nation, by this nation of "Japan," as an "Important Intangible Folk Cultural Asset." A sacred display of martial arts that, even in a peaceful age, takes the Date clan as the hypothetical enemy. That's surely how it was early in the Edo period. It was military training, a grand-scale military exercise. Hundreds of wild horses were used, and they became known as "sacred horses"; this is how the horses of Sōma could continue to live on, without their bloodline dying out. They were able to live through the 200-plus years of the Edo period.

But it's not like they could always enjoy the peace and tranquility of not being deployed. This is my second point. In Hōreki 5 and 6, which in the Western calendar is 1755–56, there was a famine, from which people died, and horses died, too. In Meiwa 6 and 7, which is 1769–70, a horrendous epidemic raged in the vicinity of Nakamura Castle, and the horses surely suffered from it as well. Then in Tenmei 3 and 4 there was an extreme famine, a tragedy that extended across the years 1783–84 and left more than 8,500 people of the Sōma fiefdom dead in its wake. The horses starved in greater numbers than the humans. Memories of that famine persist. Memories that can only be described as agonizing.

There was starvation, yes, but for the first time the horses became part of the category of "animals domesticated for food use."

Which, for the horses of Sōma, brought such frightening memories.

Anyway, I just mentioned the Nakamura Castle, without any explanation. You caught that, right? So, for my third point, I want to explain about the castle where the Sōma clan was based and the process that got them there. They started at Odaka Castle. Then in Keichō 2 they moved to Ushigoe Castle (with a name that looks like "cattle crossing"). In Keichō 8 they moved back to Odaka Castle, but in Keichō 16—which is 1611 if you work it out in the Western calendar—the Nakamura Castle was constructed. It was also called Baryō Castle (and that name means something like "horse hill"). This served as the main castle headquarters for the Sōma clan the entire time. Right up until the disappearance of the Sōma fief. The vicissitudes of this castle's history, its history of construction, affects me somehow.

What about you?

Now at the time, the Sōma fief lands only went as far as Ōkumamachi. Where we are, right now, is the southernmost tip of the Sōma clan lands. Here we are, in Ōkumamachi; what's there now?

Indeed. I wonder what is built there now.

Try starting in the twentieth century, or think of the Shōwa period: what kind of castle-building history do you find?

Now, I'm betting you have an answer to this one: nuclear power plants. There was a test run of the plant in November 1970, Shōwa 45. That would be the first of the nuclear reactors built in Fukushima. Precise name: Power Plant Number One. And I imagine you will take over from there, explaining, "the castle construction continued from there." Perhaps I should now vacate the stage. Can I look to you to take over the story from here?

That's what he said. He, this Inuzuka Gyūichirō.

We will take a break from the story here.

Our car with the Kashiwa license plates continued to make its way, its movement small in comparison. Small? Really?

Here I am writing this manuscript. Composing this essay. I must now return to the current date and time. Today is May 12.

Which brings me up, with a start, to the facts, to the reality, to the actuality: we are now past May 11.

That places us two months out from March 11. Even so, yesterday I saw hardly any news item of importance. A single month ago, on April 11, there were numerous special editions focused on "Events in the one month since March 11." And then it was on that day that I began this essay. I have now entered my second month of writing this. I have already filled more than 150 manuscript pages, no real surprise in that. I may be going a bit too fast.

But I have to wonder. Given that no major news outlets have produced investigative news stories on "Two months after the triple disasters," is my pace really too fast? To me it feels much too slow. I need to push back against the general lack of interest. I need to be inscribe this, record this. I am writing these paragraphs. Here I am, writing this manuscript.

But there is one more reason for my surprise at these facts, this situation. The turnover of the months took me by surprise. May? Was it already May? I have no recollection of encountering the end of April. Thus the fact of, the reality of, the twelfth of *May*, shocked the hell out of me.

This probably sounds ridiculous, but there is a reason for this sense of delusion. The fact of the matter is that I did not experience the end of Japan's April. Never knew the end of April in Japan. I took off from Narita on the morning of April 30, which was April 29 Eastern Standard Time, and spent the intervening hours on a plane, and got off the plane in

New York some thirteen hours later, which is to say, on the morning of April 30.

This is not about straddling two time periods. That was not my sense of things. Rather, it was about what can be contained in one calendar day, two calendar days; they stretch out, fill out; one or two days of the week can be contained in it; that kind of change. It expands, it contracts. Somewhere in that experience of time the end of Japan's April disappeared with a whoosh and a pop. Nothing I could do about it. But there in New York I did experience the night of April 30, the transition from midnight to the first moments of May 1.

By simply writing all this, by thinking about this, it came to me that this "my Japan's April" was, in its own way, a sort of being spirited-away. Yet I need to resist this phenomenon, this sense of loss. I will record and inscribe the memory that is still fresh in my mind, with this paragraph, these words. I will make it a solid memory that even I cannot alter later. I am watching two important news stories about the events of April 22 and the day before, the 21st. I am deeply touched by this human voice I hear on the TV, by the physical body that speaks those emotions, by the living flesh and blood contained in that voice, precisely because it came through the TV. The first of these images on the news was the appearance of the Fukushima Prefecture governor. He was in the prefectural government offices. The president of Tokyo Electric Company had come for a personal meeting to offer an "Apology for the Nuclear Accident." To which the

governor responded, "The children of Fukushima," he was saying, "on account of the leakage of radioactive material," he continued, "I remind you that more than six thousand of them have
no other option but to be evacuated outside the prefecture. They
have been separated from the *place where they should be.*" In these
moments it was clear, given how the mayor's voice quivered with
sadness and pain, that he was crying, although no tears fell. These
were tears that did not fall. And then the governor of Fukushima
Prefecture, outfitted in work coveralls, continued resolutely. He
went on to confront the president of Tokyo Electric Company:
"None of these nuclear power plants, neither the Fukushima
Daiichi Nuclear Power Plant nor the Fukushima Daini Nuclear
Power Plant, can ever be permitted to restart." Tears were rolling
down my face.

The second of these images is of a person whose name is
unknown to me. This man had been moved to the Tamura
city evacuation site. He shouted at the prime minister—the
prime minister of the nation of Japan, the head of the cabinet
government—on his first visit to observe the evacuation centers in Fukushima Prefecture. The prime minister had already
turned to leave after a mere ten-minute visit to the site when
the man yelled after him: "What, you're leaving already?" His
voice was clear and calm, as though designed to carry through
the evacuation center. After a space of some seconds, he spoke
again. "Are you really going to leave already?" My guess is that he
was evacuated from Katsuraomura. But it was that human voice

that effected a change in the prime minister's activities, now and into the future.

Then there is the news item that did not come through the television channels. Something I learned from the newspapers. It was announced on April 25 that twenty-eight elementary and preschools within the Kōriyama city limits would have the surfaces of their open schoolyards removed. They were going to remove of the top layer of soil on the playgrounds because they had become repositories of radioactive material. Although I didn't hear about this through newspaper reports, I later learned that heavy machinery also entered the grounds of the elementary school where I had spent six years. I imagined what it must look like. A bulldozer is scraping the open spaces of my school. Layer upon layer.

Once in America, the dates on the calendar gave me a jolt.

I am not talking about jet lag. Nor am I returning to that earlier discussion I had about what is contained in calendar days expanding and changing. I oppose calling this current catastrophe of Japan, officially known as the Great East Japan Earthquake, "3.11." This because the nuclear accident is ongoing, even after. Indeed, things got much worse after March 11. I know that people desire commemorative phrases, I get that.

But 3.11: exactly half a year later, on the other side of the world, I encountered its memorial twin: 9/11. Furthermore, America's preeminent symbol for September 11, 2001, is located in New York, home to the twin towers of the World Trade Center, a place that no longer *is*.

I am going to have to go see it, this place that has come to be called "Ground Zero." Have to. Here I am, a Japanese novelist born in this place called "Fukushima," now in New York City.

That's how it is. Although I had planned on no such thing. This trip to the U.S. had been decided last year (2010) already. At that point Japan did not yet own this 3.11 memorial number. I had been invited by Shibata Motoyuki, the scholar and translator of American literature. He is the editor of the English-language version of the literary journal called *Monkey Business*, which was scheduled to appear in April of the next year, which is to say, this spring. Since I had a piece appearing in the volume, he asked me if I would be interested in joining an event for the U.S. release. Obviously, I jumped at the chance. I thought it would be fun and exciting. He said he should be able to get appearances for me at a number of associated events.

This was all before 3.11.

Before 99 percent of Americans knew that a place called "Fukushima" even existed.

And then the event occurred in the afternoon of March 11, Japan time, and Japan came to own 3.11. I need to consider this more carefully. I figured that our entire trip would be canceled. I thought the events associated with *Monkey Business*'s English publication would never occur. I imagined a number of preliminary problems. For example, some international pilots, in the days following 3.11, refused to fly to Japan. A considerable number of countries advised their populations to "refrain from travel to Japan." "*Sakoku,*" I thought—just like that old period of national isolation when Japan's borders were closed to the outside world. Radioactive pollution, I thought, is going to drag us back into a period of isolation not seen since the Edo period 150 years ago. That is, a situation where Japanese people *leaving* their own country and *entering* another would be met with the stiffest refusal and turned away. I was thinking: should there be one or two more unexpected mishaps at the Fukushima Daiichi Nuclear Power Plant, we Japanese ourselves would be handled as radioactive material.

I could conceive of cases where external radiation, as well as internal radiation, were misdiagnosed as communicable diseases.

I could see it, at the security gates at airports around the world, the establishment of special screening stations for "Japanese only."

At the end of March and into the beginning of April I was truly gripped by this fear, this worst-case scenario. In which case, travel to New York would be impossible. But I had misjudged. The information, both domestic and international—including my own understanding of events—was changing weekly during the month of April. Speaking for myself, while I was able to avoid such extreme anxiety, things at Fukushima Daiichi—from reactors number one through four, the spent nuclear fuel, the storage pools—unfolded in a similar process. Even so, we were being told, however provisionally, that safety had been "restored."

The flight to America went without a hitch. On April 30, New York time, things were going as planned. Just one thing that disrupted the schedule: I had become, and was now, a "Fukushima" author in the post-3.11 world. That was an unexpected title. I was to appear at a bookstore in Brooklyn and also at an event in Manhattan (in the building that houses the main offices of the Japan Society). A conversation with Japanese and American authors had also been scheduled for the afternoon of April 30, the day of my arrival. The writer Kawakami Hiromi as well as the haiku master Ozawa Minoru were to appear. Of the many contributors to *Monkey Business*, we three had traveled to New York to promote it. Kawakami and Ozawa had traveled on the same flight as Shibata Motoyuki and had arrived two days earlier. I was supposed to meet the other two writers, for the first time, at the venue, but the impossible happened: we encountered each other on Lexington Avenue. I was heading south, Kawakami and the others were heading north. I think this chance encounter was indicative of the richness of our time in New York, the days of positive encounters and weighty, fecund depths. I spoke for a minute with the novelist Rebecca Brown, whom I had met in Japan before. I also spoke to the poet Joshua Beckman and was moved by the sense of his being born to create poetry. The interviewer at the Japan Society was Steve Erickson, who was just as I imagined he would be. He's the sort of person that turns out to be exactly what you would expect from his writings. The first time I met him, he had on a shirt with a print of Bob Dylan. The second time, one of Miles Davis.

Musicians, both of them.

Erickson, the Los Angeles writer who had come to New York to have this conversation with me, with musicians on his clothes.

So I appeared at those two events, and also had some interviews for magazines, and appeared on radio as well. I was invited to be on NPR by Roland Kelts, the author of *Japanamerica*. For the radio, and for the magazine articles, too, I was getting questions as a novelist from *Fukushima*. I spoke about my own questions about how I should use my imagination in the time following that 3.11 event. I tried to speak as honestly as possible, and the reactions suggest that I was rather successful. I gave three public readings. I felt I had to read publicly; I felt it important to read in my own voice. I gave two readings in Japanese and my first attempt at a reading in English. I was pleased; this seemed to be received positively. I was pleased how it seemed to be a visceral reaction, a very physical response. I felt that I was communicating. A number of good nights. I met with people, and more people, and with drinking and talking I could feel the growth of friendship.

But then, separate from all that, were the numbers.

The date.

3.11's twin, 9/11, put out an unbuffered roar. I was shaken by the howl.

This was the night of May 1. Osama bin Laden was brought down. By the U.S. (military). Precise information was, at the outset, nonexistent.

I find that I can only write this in the form of poetry.

I did not hear the voices of joy.

I did not hear the echoing chorus, in the middle of the night, there at "ground zero."

USA! USA!

I did not hear the repeated shouts.

But it happened.

That which brought such joy. That victory.

The celebration.

I went the following day.

Because, as luck would have it, I had no events scheduled for that day.

I had one completely open day.

I had someone to accompany me around the city. When we got into the taxi he said, simply, "Ground Zero."

He was an American; he was Japanese. He had dual citizenship.

I had my mouth form the words, "Ground Zero."

The place—ground—that marks the lack— zero—resulting from simultaneous terrorist attacks.

That phrase marked, of course, something different before September 11, 2001.

It marked the point of explosion for the nuclear bombs.

That was "ground zero."

On the night following the assassination of bin Laden, we arrived.

No more rubble, no more grit and dust.

A construction site.

A new symbol (a symbolic building) was being constructed.

No cries of joy.

Although they might come in future.

There were flags. There were the Stars and Stripes. And signs too: "God Bless America."

New York was a disaster site. I could see that.

But I really hadn't understood it. I had forgotten that fact.

But this disaster site, the tragedy resulting from this disaster site, I now realized:

It had an enemy.

This tragedy had a mastermind behind it.

Bin Laden.

Who could be killed.

But for us, no such thing. For us, no mastermind behind Japan's tragedy.

So then what do we do?

We have *no one we can hate.*

Which means that this is the sole source of hope.

For us, keep going, without hatred.

With no thoughts of revenge, go forward.

With no thoughts of retribution, go forward.

Words arose in my brain, of their own accord, and became voice.
They became voice. The voice spoke:
"It's OK to have been born, you know."

So it's OK to have been born. I heard a voice like a whisper. The one thing that I can do is not hate others, is to not be hateful of the world; which is to say, to adopt an attitude of love. That is what I am hoping for, that we can adopt such an attitude. The hope is like an appeal. Starting at a particular place and time of my life (perhaps I should call it my "ground zero"), I reversed my attitudes and came to love others. Like a fool. Like an absolute fool; that's fine.

And besides, I have always loved my brother and my sister. The three of us together. I loved my grandmother.

I love my father and mother. That's fine, too.

The night before leaving New York I drank quite a lot. In the hotel bar, all of us, quite a party. My English is passable, and it was sufficient to communicate. When engaged in conversation with Kawakami Hiromi and Ozawa Minoru we used Japanese, of course; the unconscious switch to English turned into a hodge-podge; a lot of fun. Joshua the poet was writing poetry in a notebook. He would write even as he was drinking. Ozawa the haiku master was also writing, he was writing things on the bar's paper napkins. Just when I began to wonder what sort of haiku he might be writing, he put the paper in my hand. It was for me, about me, a poem to capture my likeness. It read:

Moans, Quiets
Yells, Prays
Sweats

As much the sound of the words as anything. There, sung in poetry, me in New York. It was me, straight up, completely, thoroughly, me. I gave public readings, trusting the power of the unadorned voice, and he got it, all of it. With this haiku. I was moved by the power of his writing, his instincts. This poet was truly a poet, the haiku master was truly a haiku master. So what of me? For this novelist, novels.

I really did not have much free time on this trip (nothing bad about that), but I did have three or four hours that opened up. So, of course, I walked. To say that "I just walked and walked" is not metaphorical. Well, it may be a metaphor, but it also serves as something of a core tenet of my life. It's New York; one has to head for the parks. As the novice, I had to make those initial steps in Central Park. Before I entered the park I heard the sound of hooves. Horse hooves running on asphalt. Numerous horses and carriages. The sharp staccato, *tottottattattottotto*. There were also many starlings in the park. Seemed to be playing with the weeds that shot up through the grass and the dirt and the piles of fallen dried leaves. I imagine they were actually searching for insects.

Squirrels, too. And dogs being taken for walks, tens of them, hundreds of them, but they seemed slightly different in form from the dog varieties that I knew from Japan. There was a freshness in that.

Feeling a little hungry, I bought a hot dog (and a mineral water) from the cart and ate there. Many runners, many bicyclists. From there I set off toward Strawberry Fields. There is a spot in Central Park clearly marked with a sign. Strawberry Fields is, of course, at least as far as I know, the name of an orphanage. It was located in England, in Liverpool, the port city that looks out onto the Irish Sea, and the source of the imagination that went into the Beatles' "Strawberry Fields Forever," to be sung into eternity, forever. I sang it as well. And the characters in my novel, the brothers in *The Holy Family*, sang it too.

It was a place to remember John Lennon.

It was a monument. At the spot where three walking paths meet each other is a mosaic. I found out later that it was designed by Yoko Ono.

But of course. John was shot in New York. In 1980. Four years before that he had received his permanent residency for the United States.

The novel was calling; I knew it. My novel was calling me. So I returned to Fukushima. From here, with this essay as well, I return to Fukushima. I will skip the return to Japan. A description of that event is not necessary. I am still in that small car with the Kashiwa license plate. With young S, with Ms. S, and with Y. I had now visited the Hamadōri section of Fukushima, the north side of the meltdown, but I had not yet seen the south side of the meltdown. I had not yet gone toward the border of Ibaraki Prefecture; not yet felt the southern tip of Fukushima Prefecture in my skin, so had to make our way from there north through Iwaki City.

We came upon the old barrier gate at Nakoso. It was on a hill. The Nakoso barrier gate, together with that other famous barrier at Shirakawa, has often appeared in traditional poetry. In short, this spot marks the beginning of the *michinoku*—the lands beyond the pale, the deep north. Both are poetic *utamakura*, places often sung of in traditional poetry. While lingering in the area, we heard the cry of a nightingale.

We had arrived via the Jōban expressway. Seven or eight kilometers after exiting at the Iwaki-Nakoso highway interchange. In the morning of the day following our time in Shinchimachi, then Sōma, and Minami Sōma; that following morning. On our way to the gate at Nakoso we stopped at a convenience store. The first convenience store we had stopped at in Iwaki.

They were short on supplies.

We had arrived at our destination, but the fact is that no one can say with certainty that this is the actual location of the Nakoso barrier gate. Some authorities place it here; that's all that can be said. The simple fact of the matter is that we were standing in a park that commemorates the barrier gate. There were innumerable memorial stones, the kind with poems engraved on them, some might say too many: stele engraved with *waka* poems, tablets engraved with the lines of famous poets like Ki no Tsurayuki, Ono no Komachi, and Izumi Shikibu, a veritable forest of them.

And then a haiku by Matsuo Basho.

Lines of different poems, numerous stanzas.

The name "Nakoso" is said to mean "Do not come here, you northern barbarians." According to one explanation, anyway. Many unexplained aspects of the border between Ibaraki and Fukushima Prefectures remain. What we know is that there used to be an ancient border in this area (or an area understood to be a border), a place, for example, that separated the Hitachi and Mutsu lands, which meant it delineated the Tohoku and Kanto regions. The two were distinctly separated here; there is no doubt about that. "Do not come here, you Yi barbarians from the north." This phrase can be translated with another layer of meaning: "You people from *Tohoku*, you indigenous peoples from *up there*, do not come down here to *our Kanto*."

A heavy warning.

Even so, it is a tourist area, now a park. I listened intently for the song of the nightingale. I felt nothing else. The Izumi Shikibu poem struck me as very fine, however.

We returned to the parking lot and drove down from the hill. The park housed a museum devoted to literature related to the Nakoso barrier gate, but it was closed. A sign was on the door; it said simply, "Museum temporarily closed." The building showed no fractures or damage. All the various sites related to the gate, and all the memorial tablets, seemed to have escaped damage from the earthquake. At least as far as we could tell, anyway.

Route 6, on which we were traveling, hugs the shoreline; the route is known locally, of course, as the Rikuzen Beach Highway. The JR Jōban line runs parallel. This on the Pacific Ocean side. This is the Pacific side of Fukushima Prefecture, its southern tip. The Nakoso beach was visible through the right-hand window, I could see it by looking over the shoulder of Y, who was sitting next to me. But all the damage wrought by the tsunami, the terrible damage reported on, was not verifiable by the eye. Perhaps a fortunate accident of local geography. Given the shape of the bay, the beach.

But there is one detail here that I cannot fail to explain.

Shortly after we left—I mean immediately after—for a number of days on end, Hamadōri was rocked by aftershocks. On April 7 there was a major tremor that registered a strong 6 in Miyagi Prefecture, a strong 5 in Hamadōri. Then in the evening of April 11, a weak 6. A little after noon on the following day, the twelfth, a weak 6. As far as I can tell by looking at the map (the map recording the shock epicenters), the epicenter was directly underneath the barrier gate at Nakoso. For nearly all of the shocks.

The Jōban expressway was closed because of landslides. This was on the stretch of road that we had driven, in the area where we had been. The damage caused by those aftershocks resulted in a number of deaths.

This morning (the morning of May 14) brought another major shock with the epicenter just off the Fukushima coast. It registered a 4 in Hamadōri. In Iwaki City, also 4.

I have to write these things down.

Visualizations. Those poetic memorial stones, I wonder how they fared. Wonder if the poems have crumbled.

Off to the side was the Nakoso beach. I could see it over Y's shoulder, just beyond his head. Just a momentary glimpse, but a surprising scene. A fitness center was there, the building still intact, with all the treadmills still lined up and facing the sea. It appeared to still be open for business. It addled my brain: quietly, calmly waiting there for the ocean, a phantom fitness club patiently waiting for the ocean to come, all those phantom indoor runners.

I probably should have asked young S, who was driving, to pull over to the side of the road, just for a moment. Because, just maybe, *this was not a phantom*. But we had already driven past. We continued north on National Highway 6. We were heading for the port at Onahama. The car navigation system on the dashboard continued to receive radio broadcasts and was playing the

NHK news. Inside the car. It was now eleven a.m. The main news story was about the current situation at Fukushima Daiichi. While listening to that we were making our way smoothly, one kilometer, two kilometers, ever closer to the meltdown. As you would expect, the four of us found ourselves wrapped in unusual sensations. Then there was the surprise attack—there can be no other word for it. Given our experiences in the northern part of Fukushima Prefecture, in Shinchimachi in the northernmost part, we should have been prepared for a shocking landscape, but weren't; we were ambushed.

We did not continue straight on Onahama road but turned off to the right. We were headed toward the docks and the fishing piers. It was immediately clear that this was all reclaimed land, a factory district where all the company names and signs displayed their business of smelting or galvanizing or chemical works. It looked to me exactly the same as the harbor areas of Tokyo, with the same stench (that came to me instinctively, before thought). We saw what we should have known to expect but were still surprised. The tragedy of reclaimed land, now reduced to a lique-fied state. This is what happens when a major earthquake attacks a large reclaimed area. Reclaimed areas are built on landfill, so the foundations are rather weak. There was extensive damage, some that was abstract, some following geometrical patterns. For example, the manholes and the manhole covers and the under-ground conduits attached to them were, here and there, sticking out of the ground. At some places sticking up a few centimeters, at others, ten or twenty. And we found many areas where the sand and the water gushed out together. Clearly, a large expanse of area had been ravaged by high-pressure water shooting out from the depths of the earth, the result of the earthquakes. The entire area was liquefied.

But such ravages. First there was the major earthquake. The four of us in the car, breathless and fearful, made our way along the docks. At one traffic intersection the scene spread before us looked as though the earthquake, in all its self-centered ego-tism, had no thought but to try its destructive energy and test everything, to see, "Will this shake too?" I felt this scene had been lying in wait for us, to gnaw at our very souls. Ms. S was in the passenger seat; she told young S, who was driving, to turn right toward the shoreline. Dock Number 2. One of the largest aquariums in Tohoku was located there. "Aquamarine Fukushima." It was *still* there, but vehicles could not enter. So we joined the handful of cars parked in a line by the side of the road, and stopped the car with Kashiwa license plates. A sign-board proclaimed, "The aquarium is temporarily closed today." A very proper professional signboard. A movable barrier had been placed there to prevent vehicles from entering. It had a handwrit-ten sign attached to it: "Unauthorized persons forbidden entry"

I knew this already. The aquarium had been temporarily closed since March 11; the work of rescuing the many varieties of fish was ongoing, but the reality of it was exceedingly sad. Authorized aquarium employees still came, struggling hard,

never losing hope as they continued their work. The large sea
animals had been relocated to various aquariums. I wonder what
happened to the penguins; I think of them as birds. I stared
from the distance at the looming cathedral-like aquarium building. Wondered what had been damaged exactly, and where. The
walkway that started off to the side of the "entry forbidden" barrier also showed scars from the earthquake.

"Let's walk," I said. To Y, to Ms. S, to young S.

We walked from Dock Number 2 toward Dock Number 1.
I would like to insert our conversation here, but the fact is that
we hardly exchanged any words. In an e-mail he sent me after we
got back to Tokyo, young S called it "temporary aphasia." In that
moment, we could not express even that. We had no means to do
so. We had no means, no words, but we looked. Dock Number
1 has a big public building called "Iwaki la la myuu" connected
by a pier, a kind of boardwalk. Sections had caved in. The planks
from the wooden flooring had been ripped up, the concrete was
cracked, broken into pieces, deplorable, caved-in. The tiles and
the tile-like material on the walkways had popped up. Plucked
by an excessive force and strewn around. Along the back side of
the boardwalk were a number of small storehouses, now clearly
hollowed out and filled with nothing, clearly announcing: "We
stand here empty." Missing walls, fallen beams and pillars, not a
soul around. Over in the Iwaki la la myuu area, to the standhold-
ers' entrance, and to the place that clearly should have had a plate
glass window, someone had hastily affixed sheets of plywood,

communicating a clear message to me, to all of us: "Off limits." The boats for tourists were tied up on the western side of the pier, bobbing, bobbing on the surface of the water. That didn't seem so odd. A little farther on, right at the head of Dock Number 1, stood two big ships, next to each other.

But they were on land.

The ships had not moved. That did seem odd.

Really, can this be possible, to move them to land, and leave them there, is that really OK?

The awareness drums itself into my head in staccato. Similarly the name of the building, Iwaki la la myuu, which carries in its name this staccato. We turn the corner at the head of the pier to find the terminal for the tourist boats. The main doors are closed off with a number of sheets of plywood. I look and register three facts: (1) it is completely closed off; (2) no one is going to depart from here by ship; (3) no tourist boats are going to arrive. What has arrived here is the March 11 tsunami. Only that massive wave of water; after that, nothing.

The tsunami wave swallowed up this area. The thought did not have to form, I could see it. And the devastating damage it wrought. Piles of cracked asphalt. Cracked? Ripped up? Here and there empty spaces, hollowed-out spaces. What used to be here were the fisheries facilities, or what look to be stands for the market. The "myuu" of "la la myuu" probably refers to the "*myuu*" of museum, but there is no sense that this museum dedicated to water and ocean, to fishing and shipping, even exists or is open.

We returned to the warehouse area. Y found a water faucet and twisted the spigot open, but no water. Of course not.

Maybe it was just emptiness pouring out.

On the ground of the entrance to one of the storehouses (an area of poured concrete) fat spikes were sticking out about ten centimeters in a line, suspended as though trying to extricate themselves. Was this the work of the earthquake? Or perhaps of the liquefaction of the earth? Maybe just the sport of the tsunami, throwing its power around. At any rate, I was looking out onto a scene that should not be possible, a situation that should not be. In the area around Docks Number 1 and 2, and in the deck area between them and the warehouse area were crows, only crows. These are not birds (鳥) I am talking about, but crows (烏). Just like we saw in Shinchimachi and Minami Sōma, the carrion crows that gathered here; no other varieties of birds were to be seen. Compared to the large-billed crows I am used to seeing in Tokyo, these—not just the bills—are thin of body, and their movements also seem thinner. We got back into our Kashiwa car and moved less than a kilometer. Off to the pier at Onahama, to the area where we expected to find the fish market and fisheries cooperative. We were assaulted by a sense that there could be no time more suitable than now for the phrase "what should not be," the impossible. Up on the dock, here, in the exact opposite of orderliness, the fishing boats, many, many ships, big and small, were jumbled and leaning against one another. Of course, they had been pushed up by the tsunami. "Stacked in a pile" was the first impression. But who, what hand, is able to stack ships in this way? Further, they were arranged, slanted in all sorts of directions. No, they had arranged themselves. I looked. Up on the land, the bow and stern, the rudders and screw propellers.

Wondering if it is appropriate to go in for a closer look.

And stand next to them?

But it was impossible.

In such a completely unnatural situation I could not grasp the overwhelming power of the steel. Even though I might be crushed by it at any moment. By the entire twisted mass. Y was taking pictures. Young S was around somewhere. And Ms. S? It had progressed to the point where even the communal sense of the experience shared among us (shared in this space) was impossible. There was no way, we lacked the means, the know-how. But we watched. Four people's eyes, eight retinas. I found a phone booth, I stepped into the glass box. The phone was silver but streaked with mud. The phone number, which I assume was a special kind of phone number, was Onahama 000260. I picked up the receiver, felt its weight. But I couldn't bring it to my ear. One of my eardrums does not function.

We went back to highway 6. After a late lunch, we decided to continue north. We resolved to get as close as possible to the thirty-kilometer exclusion zone around the Fukushima Daiichi Plant. We headed toward the Yotsukura section of Iwaki City.

Farther up the road are Hironomachi, Narahamachi, Tomio-kamachi, Ōkumamachi. We know that they are *there*, but we won't go that far. Even so, we proceed about ten or fifteen kilometers out of Onahama. The four of us in our little rental car are running along the Pacific coast. Who is it that calls this "Fukushima's East Coast?" Tourist guidebooks would. Guide-books from before these horrifying three-layered natural/human disasters. We had easily made it about twenty kilometers out of Onahama, but we couldn't go thirty. We may not even have left Onahama. We were trying to get as far as the arc demarcating the thirty-kilometer perimeter, but we found ourselves stuck at that point where Route 6 meets Prefectural Route 41, what is known locally as the Ono Yotsukura Highway. The police had it blockaded. This was because the earthquake or the tsunami had rendered the highways "impassable," not, apparently, on account of the meltdown or the evacuation zone. At any rate, we couldn't proceed. We turned toward the coastline. This was not Yotsu-kura Port. This was the entrance to Yotsukura beach. The Yotsu-kura Port rest stop was just ahead; I was thinking to myself how the Hattachi shoreline was just another three or four kilometers farther on (all along here Route 6 ran in parallel to the JR Jōban train line, each coming close to touching the other before plung-ing forward together into the thirty-kilometer arc), but I could not hope for what cannot be. We got out of the car and started walking between the fishing port and the beach area. We began to hear the sounds of waves and headed toward the beach. A line of concrete tetrapod breakwater structures was visible on the nonbeach side. Perfectly white. I saw them, a "flock" of tetrapods. The seabirds were crying. I could see on the beach palms that had clearly been transplanted, sparsely arranged. I searched the horizon for the seabirds, but all that was visible in the landscape, near and far, were the carrion crows loitering on the embankments. Young S was off in the distance, smoking a cigarette. Y, who until a moment ago was right next to me, was also off in some other section, doing something. I was walking with Ms. S. Her shadow fell on the sand. Far, far at the distant water's edge, literally off in the distance, I realized, "There are the seagulls." Seagulls? We walked farther. That walk certainly felt like a "forward progression." It was an unusual shallow area of wide shoals. As we walked along, the farther we walked, the more clearly we could recognize how large a group of seabirds was out there. I am not talking about a hundred birds. Must have been two hundred, three hundred. It would probably have taken an experienced birdwatcher to accurately estimate the number; it was an unusually large gathering. The smell of the sea was getting stronger and more oppressive; I licked my finger as a test. Salty. Sticking to the skin, the salt breeze. I pulled out my camera and removed the lens cap. Intent on being as quick as possible in order to not expose the lens to the salt breeze, I raised the camera. The group of birds. Pointed it toward the massive gathering of birds. That's when Ms. S said, "Those gulls are called sea cats, aren't they?"

Ten of them took off into flight.

Followed by ten more.

Circling in the air.

A flash of recognition. Someone said, "Come over here!" I heard the voice in my head. There was a simple overlap of that commanding voice and a song melody. A song that took me back. A song that felt very close to me, and to someone other than me as well, close to those brothers as well. A Beatles song. One that contains the musical effect that sounds like a seagull cry. I thought to myself, heard myself ask, "The song with the seagull cry, which song was that, brother, do you know?"

"Come over here."

"Listen, you hear the Beatles' 'Tomorrow Never Knows,' don't you?"

"Do you know who I am? This is Inuzuka Gyūichirō. Listen, I am talking to you now. You need a story, right?"

"The continuation of the story that I interrupted awhile ago."

"Yes. My brother disappeared, but I am still here."

What I heard from him ends there. The rest I will write myself. I write of the Gyūichirō after the disappearance of his brother, the Gyūichirō of *The Holy Family*, the eternal elder brother Inuzuka Gyūichirō. What is possible for people like him, people who exist in a dimension outside time? It was as though he could see into a deep pool, the depths of history. It was as though he could see it in concentrated form, all of existence submerged under the surface of that water. Then he would dive in. He could swim in deep water. Even so, he was not some sort of time traveler in a science-fiction novel. That sort of notion did not exist within him. He was simply a migrant with a physical voice, bearing the burden of blood, lamentations, and a murderous past. And deformed fists. The place where he "was" is a place that actually "is." For example, he is within the precincts of a Shinto shrine—could be any shrine, although it is one of the ones in the Sōma region. But what divides the inner precincts, and what falls outside the shrine grounds (the outer world)? Torii, that's what. The gate known as torii. A symbol unique to Japan, of "Shinto," the religion and common belief system.

One enters through the torii, one leaves through the torii; no different than customs and immigration checkpoints.

One crosses into the domain of the gods, one leaves again; exactly like the activities that require passports, immigration and customs clearances, and security checks. But here the recognized passport is engraved on one's spirit. Thus, no matter where he is in history, every time he is on the grounds of a shrine and he passes under a torii, his spirit is examined. A positive match of spirit and individual: "We can see that you are who you say you are." And at the same time his murderous past is deemed a match to the murderous past of the "nation." (I beg the reader's indulgence for my dramatic turn of phrase.) A verdict is handed down.

So he moves on to the next place. He is essentially expelled, from one space to another. The phenomenon works like this: from the shrine precincts where he "is," he passes through the torii, to subsequently appear on the grounds of another shrine. He passes through the torii and ends up "there."

This is the movement between spaces. However, if the destination shrine happens to be in a different "point in time," there is also a change in the temporal dimension. There were shrines in the Kamakura period; there were shrines in the Sengoku period before the Edo period (which also includes the Azuchi Momoyama period); there were also shrines at the beginning, middle, and end of the Edo period. So it goes without saying that the numerous, nearly infinite torii of the shrines of the Sōma fief serve as gates at the border separating these dimensions.

I will stop here with the theorizing. Same with my efforts to shore up the logic. I just want to write. I want to write what I have seen. I want to describe the scene that "exists" in my head, capturing it with all the internal urgency I feel. In this endeavor my imagination becomes the driving force. But is such imagination a good thing?

I write, "He is here."

Doesn't matter which shrine, as long as it is in the Sōma region, and one of the more prestigious ones. Not a contemporary shrine. Not the grounds of a present-day shrine, in 2011, in Heisei 23; Well, what era then? It would be the Sengoku period. There is a horse pasture on the precincts, surrounded by a fence.

A number of horses. He is talking to one of them. He, Gyūichirō, asks, "So, are you a mare?"

"Yesss"—is not exactly an answer the horse can provide, but in fact it is a mare.

"Have you returned from the battlefield? From a little joust with the sworn enemy, the Date clan?"

"Yesss"—is not an answer the horse can give, but that is accurate. This horse did not lose her life on the battlefield and she has now been returned to the Sōma holdings. However, her "rider" was not so lucky. The samurai on her back was first struck by arrows then beheaded with helmet still intact, and remained in the saddle, but now as a corpse, for miles and miles, for untold hours. He was able to discern all this and proceeded to question the horse with a sympathetic tone.

"Making your way through the engagement with the enemy armies with a dead man strapped to your back, was no doubt very difficult. Was it difficult for you?"

"Yesss, yes, yes," the horse was able to answer through a whinny. He heard the answer quite clearly. He was stroking her neck, and he continued speaking: "But you came back alive. And before long you will become pregnant, give birth, and all will take its turns within the fullness of time. I see that this will come to pass, and I celebrate with you."

And with that, this Inuzuka Gyūichirō turned to the path leading through the shrine and passed under the torii. And with that he appeared at a different shrine, on the path under a

different torii. This shrine could also be said to exist in the Sengoku world but was already in the Azuchi Momoyama period.
Further, it was immediately after the siege of Odawara Castle.
When Toyotomi Hideyoshi had forced the Hōjō clan to capitu-
late, which was in Tenshō 18 (1590). The horse he had met in the
pasture had returned from this battle. A female. He continued
with his questioning. He was still stroking her. "In this battle
you had to carry the dead soldiers, didn't you, the warriors. But
this will be healed," he proclaimed. He promised that he would
keep an eye on her on into the future. With that he passed again
through the torii. And he appeared on shrine grounds in another
time period and encountered there a horse of the Sōma domain
in the throes of the famine of the Hōreki years. That despair and
fear—the fear of starvation—he listened to and he assuaged. The
next torii he passed through took him into the Tenmyō years.
Despite an even more severe famine, the horses were being kept
alive because they had to participate in the Sōma clan Nomaoi
festival. He met with a group of mares that somehow had managed to live through this. "You," he began, "you will be outlived
by offspring, to fill this side of time, I will see to it."

He promised. He moved on.

At the end of the Tokugawa period, the horses had no worries.
The horses lived through the span of the Meiji period. And the
Taishō period as well. There was one crisis in the Shōwa period;
this relates to the war that is connected to world history (the
Second World War), but they were living. Then comes the end

of the Shōwa period. The reign name changes to Heisei. In the twenty-third year of that era, he appeared on the grounds of a shrine that exists now, in the present.

This was in the Sōma area, deep in the southern part.

There are no people. It has become deserted. Everyone has been ordered to evacuate. "Leave." "You must depart this ground." "But this only applies to you humans." These the words from the government of this nation, "Japan."

One white horse was there. The horse was emaciated. Its ribcage was visible. It was near starvation. Food was clearly insufficient. Still in the pasture, it had not been freed. He walked up to it. He called out to it. He said, "You are the offspring of all those horses," he said this with tears streaming down his cheeks. Tears dropping, dropping, one after the other. And then he did what he could.

He threw open all the gates.

At which point he disappears from the story. What remains now is the tale of the horse. One male horse, a starving white horse. A white horse that is on the loose. Searching for grass, walking free. Grass, he found. If one must decide whether he is a Western breed or a Japanese breed, in the stomach of this horse that has been "Westernized" such grasses and plants are hard to digest, but he ate nonetheless. The world is devoid of people; walking is now the only thing that the white horse can do. In the morning, a beautiful sky. And at noon, a clear blue sky. At night, dark and cold. For the first two or three days, no rain falls.

The horse has no idea that the rain, even should it fall, would be mixed with radioactive material. It simply registers its dislike of the cold. But the weather has its cycles, and a clear-skied morning returns again. A beautiful light, clear and transparent, that makes one feel the height of the heavens. At the edge of the field of vision run a number of cattle. A group of five or six. They too have been let loose, allowed to run free. But since, in fact, they are no longer being cared for, this is more like being "abandoned to" the range.

And at an even farther remove, people.

The humans are white. They are wearing white protective clothing to ward off radioactivity, covered in white cloth from the tops of their heads. The white horse unconsciously runs the other way. People who look like that are frightening. They may in fact be Fukushima prefectural police enacting the protection and care of those in the area (including reporting on the "stray" horses), but to the eye they are completely white, plus they have Geiger counters at their sides. They are frightening.

The horse did not meet any dogs. Dogs that used to be pets are now wild.

There were a number of crushed cars. In places, the fragrance of incense. Someone's death being commemorated. Perhaps this was right after the Self-Defense Forces broadscale search for bodies throughout the "evacuation zone." But these were not the thoughts of the white horse. The tractors that were turned upside-down on the asphalt struck him as unnatural, however. But the white horse walked on, continued forward. He came upon an elementary school, entered the grounds, but no sounds of children were to be heard, and the gymnasium was also vacant, and he understood that all of this had been abandoned. The white horse walked as far as the first-floor entrance to the school buildings. He saw the wall clock hanging there. The hands were still.

The white horse continued to look for edible grasses.

He came upon a small building. It was the cow barn for a dairy herd. The door for the domestic-animal shed had been opened by the proprietor at the time of evacuation. So the cows—mothers and calves—had been given their freedom. The fact is that few were inside the shed, but often one or two were there. The cows used the shed as a base, freely wandering the nearby area, returning to the shed at regular intervals. They spent time inside the fence and outside the fence, on something of a fixed schedule. But one day there was a massive aftershock. At precisely that moment there was one female black cow (a mother) inside the shed, and the force of the level 5 aftershock closed the gate, locking the latch tight. If pulled from the inside, it is easily opened but a cow has no means to pull. Has no means, has no arms. So she fell into the dangerous state of being trapped. More than ten days passed. She was starving to death. Completely thin.

This is what the white horse found. He could sense another living being; even so, he did not run away. Perhaps out of simple curiosity, perhaps out of hope that a cow shed might hold food, he pushed on the door and entered.

He pushed on it. He pushed on it, and it opened. Quite simple.

And he met the eye of the cow.

The white horse understood that there was nothing to be had there and proceeded back outside. With that, the thin and emaciated cow tottered after. The white horse paid no attention and continued forward, walked steadily on. The cow followed after, in earnest, as hard as she could, toward the nearby embankment covered in bright green grass. The white horse began eating the grass; off to the side, and a little later, the cow, too, was eating.

All the grasses were gaining nourishment from the light. Light was falling, sunlight.

About three kilometers to the east of this is the shoreline. The seabirds are calling. But nothing is dying. Death definitely exists, but in this moment, death is not at work.

And at this point my essay ends, and begins.

Translator's Afterword

FURUKAWA Hideo's *Horses, Horses, in the End the Light Remains Pure: A Tale That Begins with Fukushima* (*Umatachi yo, sore demo hikari wa muku de*) was among the first major literary responses to the triple disasters—the earthquake, tsunami, and subsequent nuclear meltdown—that occurred in northeast Japan on March 11, 2011. The work was published in its entirety in the journal *Shinchō* in July 2011 and almost immediately thereafter in book form—four months, that is, after the earthquake/tsunami/meltdown known in Japan as 3.11. It has become a touchstone for discussion of literature in the aftermath. And, as those reading this afterword *after* reading the work now know, it is compelling and important for all the reasons that it can be exasperating and demanding. *Horses, Horses* is a sort of memoir, sort of fiction, sort of essay, something of a road trip; it can be chaotic and overwhelming.

While Furukawa bristles at being labeled a "Fukushima writer," the fact that this work chronicles a return through the Fukushima prefectural towns of his childhood, where his family still lives, adds another dimension to the stories being told. It is hard to overstate the effect of the cataclysms marked by 3.11. It is also worth being reminded that March 11 marks only the beginning point of the disasters, not the end, as they are not contained. The effects of radiation and displacement, the disruption of lives, will continue for decades, for centuries. *Horses, Horses* reflects the fallout from the disasters: raw, sometimes confused, convoluted and multilayered, forceful, personal, just like the disasters and the responses of those caught up in them. It captures the sense that all the important things of a day before—all the major novels to be written, for example—were suddenly proved meaningless, ephemeral, and, somehow, devoid of importance. Further, *Horses, Horses* captures the sensibility that 3.11 marked a "before" or "after," a feeling that has diminished considerably in the years since but seemed impossible to doubt in 2011.

Horses, Horses recounts the shock of the disasters, made the more distressing to the Furukawa narrator because he was not at home when they struck and therefore feels more keenly the tenuousness of communication and connections. Some phone calls got through and some did not; like everyone, he found himself unable to stop watching the scenes as they played across screens and monitors. On March 11, Furukawa's farming family was in Fukushima prefecture when the disasters struck; Furukawa, who is based in Tokyo, was in Kyoto gathering materials for a novel. So this is not the tale of a Tohoku native who watched friends and neighbors, buildings, and everything else be washed out to sea only to then be haunted by real but invisible radiation: there are many of those. Rather, one of the important strains of this work is its recounting of the other common experience of contemporary Japan: living the surreal experience of physics-defying images unfolding across innumerable screens, being caught up in scenes that should not be: ships on roads, boats on schools, waves surging through rice fields. An early image of the novel replicates this: eyes that should close but cannot, will not. The work is haunted by guilt and paralysis; it is driven by a real-time record of coming to terms with the devastation. Further, it records the author's compulsion from outside, beckoning and demanding, that he "go there," but the path leading to the "there" is oblique, multidimensional, multivocal. This unspecified voice is consistent throughout: "go," "see," "write." The "ground zero" of time is marked by the beginning point of a restart, a reboot.

Horses, Horses opens in media res of another Furukawa novel. *Seikazoku* (The holy family), the *other* novel (as it is often referred to), is a sprawling work that traces the convoluted story of two brothers as they meander through the Tohoku region, the same region, that is, of Furukawa's family lineage and the 3.11 disasters, the " 'North' plus 'east' [that] adds up to Tohoku." *Holy Family* was completed and in print years before March 2011, but it was clearly still much on the mind of the author. The earlier novel is so insistent that the brothers of *Seikazoku* appear as characters in *Horses, Horses*; one shows up in the back seat of Furukawa's car as he makes his way north from Tokyo to Tohoku. The brothers' story simultaneously traces contours of Japan's northeast, of Tohoku, both in *Horses, Horses* and in *Seikazoku*. This is one way that the atmosphere of *Horses, Horses* is thick with multiple voices and challenging perspectives. The work conflates temporalities and voices, time and space. It also reflects the fierce history of a rugged region in the shadow of the national, urban, controlling capital of Tokyo. The brothers' story of disaster and mayhem, which overlaps with violent histories of the region, weaves depth into the experience of the 3.11 disasters and their relationship to this region.

Horses, Horses is also driven by the bloody tales the region has to tell of nonhuman actors, as the title leads us to expect. Horses, especially, but dogs, cows, and birds—like Furukawa's family, like the brothers of *Seikazoku*—are all disrupted, all share histories and parallel stories, all have been pushed under or cut out by the centers of power. We encounter many of these varied characters in the opening scene: human beings, the narrator, the presence of extraterrestrials, the brothers from *Seikazoku*, the sense of place signified by Tohoku. Likewise, at the outset we encounter the concern for dates and calendars, for ancient tales, for alternate tellings, concern, that is, for ownership of one's own history and narrative.

The fact that all of the electric output from the Fukushima Nuclear plant was destined for Tokyo—indeed, the power plant is administered not by any local entity but by Tokyo Electric Power Company, which means that the most insidious changes from the radiation, which affect every aspect of the living beings of Fukushima, are caused solely by and for Tokyo—becomes a touchstone for the entire work. It drives the sense of injustice;

it drives the ferreting out of stories, for example, not just the histories of humans, but the histories of horses: Horses are historical actors and characters here; horses are constituent of the place names of this affected region; horses are evacuated following the disasters; horses are traumatized; horses are in temporary shelters. The Furukawa narrator's travel unearths the history of horses in community and of horses being slaughtered at the whims of central-governmental powers across the centuries. This, of course, parallels the histories of humans in the region. The disasters of 3.11 and the Furukawa narrator's traveling through the region in the aftermath become the stimulus for those narratives. Such histories add an entirely different narrative line to the tale; it is another of the ways in which this is much more than a 3.11 narrative.

In terms of style, Furukawa's long involvement in theater is evident in his forceful and engaging dramatic readings. Further, the effusive maximalist writing style (by which I mean more Dave Eggers or Jonathan Safran Foer than Ann Beattie or Silas House, to draw examples from my own bookshelf) seems designed to engage the range of human cognition. Furukawa and his writing are electric and multifocused. They bristle with energy; they unfold in multiple dimensions. He writes prolifically across genres. Science fiction, magical realism, fantasy, as well as oral storytelling traditions are all evident here, as are his concerns for the various regions and histories, the panoply of living creatures, and the variety of narratives from across Japan.

Furukawa has become particularly engaged with histories, memory work, and commemoration in the aftermath of 3.11. For example, while he was writing *Horses, Horses*, he was undertaking a rewrite and retelling,[1] in theater and film, of Miyazawa Kenji's *Night on the Milky Way Railroad*. Furukawa draws much from Miyazawa Kenji (1896–1933), the elliptic, multilayered, hard-to-characterize poet and storyteller from Iwate Prefecture in northeastern Japan, who was born in the year of another great tsunami. Their shared regional base, and the experience of inundating waters, anchors a sense of common purpose and narrative ground. Furukawa's rewrite of Miyazawa's widely loved *Night on the Milky Way Railroad* provides the script for the *Hontō no uta* (*True Songs*) dramatic-reading-cum-theatrical-performance that has been staged throughout Japan and internationally.[2] The use of literary activity as intervention is also evident in the workshop Furukawa organizes in Tohoku under the name of "A Drifting Classroom" (Tadayo manabiya). The classroom is designed for participants to explore, through "literature," the individual narratives that have arisen in response to the disasters.[3]

All of which is to say that Furukawa is one of the most imaginative and prolific of contemporary Japanese writers. He was awarded the Mystery Writers of Japan Association Prize and the Japan SF Grand Prize for *Tribes of the Arabian Nights* (*Arabia no yoru no shūzoku*) in 2002 and the Mishima Yukio Prize for *LOVE* in 2004; he published the massive *Seikazoku* in 2008; *Onnatachi no sanbyakunin no uragirusho* (The book of the womens' 300 betrayals; 2015) is a remix of the *Tale of Genji*, the thousand-year-old tale of exploits and affairs at court; and he is currently translating the *Tale of Heike*, that classic of medieval war tales, into contemporary Japanese.

NOTES

1. The "re-" prefix is important to Furukawa—rewrites are often remixes, reworkings, or reorganizations of the source text. They are also, as is especially evident in the case of *Horses, Horses*, to be understood as a restart, a reboot, a zero point that marks a new beginning.
2. The performance, which has been recorded in a documentary film, includes poet and translator Suga Keijirō, one of the forces behind the project; the musician Kojima Keitaney Love; and the translator Motoyuki Shibata. See http://milkyway-railway.com.
3. http://www.tadayoumanabiya.com/index.php#outline.

Translator's Acknowledgments

FIRST, thanks go to Akiko Takenaka, who has been through every line, most more than once. Likewise, I am humbled by the careful reading and cogent feedback, again, on every line, by Rachel DiNitto, Davinder Bhowmik, and Shibata Motoyuki. I acknowledge the changes prompted by discussions with the students of JPN 421—too many to mention by name. I thank Suga Keijirō for being, in many ways, the impetus and catalyst for the project. Thanks go to Columbia University Press—especially to Jennifer Crewe, Jonathan Fiedler, and Michael Haskell—for their commitment to this project and the accelerated timeline. I also thank Furukawa Hideo for his enthusiasm and availability for the conundrums of the text, and Furukawa Chie for her support as well.

Excerpts, in different form, appeared in *Words Without Borders* as "Spirited Away: Hideo Furukawa's 'Horses, Horses, in the Innocence of Light,'" parts 1 and 2, March 11 and 12, 2015, http://www.wordswithoutborders.org/dispatches/article/spirited-away-hideo-furukawas-horse-horses-in-the-innocence-of-light. An excerpt, in different form, appeared in *The Asia-Pacific Journal: Japan Focus*, vol. 13, issue 10, no. 3, March 16, 2015.